SHADE KISSED

PHOENIX RISING BOOK FOUR

ANNIE ANDERSON

SHADE KISSED
Phoenix Rising Book 4

International Bestselling Author
Annie Anderson
Copyright © 2017 Annie Anderson
Print ISBN: 978-1-960315-24-3

Editing by Barb Shuler & Emily Maynard
Cover Art & Formatting by Tattered Quill Designs

www.annieande.com

For those of you who saw the beauty and determination of Nicola long before I did. This is for you.

PROLOGUE

NICOLA—BEFORE

I NEVER SAW HIM COMING.

Just my luck, I suppose, I would find my love when I knew I wasn't long for this world.

Getting a mate before my inevitable end seemed like a horrible thing at first, but I couldn't help the slight niggles of happiness which broke through the wall around my heart.

I'd built that wall myself out of the broken promises and lies told to me in my youth. It kept me safe—staved off the loneliness and heartbreak—but it didn't keep him out.

My visions all but dried up nearly a month ago, but I knew from all the ones before Iva worked the forbidden magic which damned my sight I wasn't going to make it. Three centuries seemed so long and so short all at the same time. How could I have had so much time on this earth and wasted it? Is this what humans feel like when approached with a terminal illness? Do they lament the time they spent on trivial matters and wish they'd done more?

Do they have so much regret?

Everything I'd done, every single atrocity and willful neglect—all of the things I could have prevented, the lives I could have saved—made me the worst sort of person. But I did them all knowing I was saving my race. Sure, I had dirt under my nails, but all my toils wouldn't be for nothing.

I hoped.

Time was speeding by, and I wanted to experience everything I'd been denied. I wasn't going to feel the perfection of an evil put to death or the purity of wrongs being righted. I wasn't going to see my greatest sin washed from my soul. But I could have a little bit of happiness before I went, and with my plan in place and the first domino about to fall... Time was a luxury I no longer had.

Then, he came along with his hulking presence and soft, rumbling voice and death seemed like a blessing and a curse. A blessing because I hadn't had much happiness in my life and he seemed like a gift given to me at the very last second. But a curse as well because I wasn't going to get to keep him. I didn't deserve him and I never would, and the burn of losing him—even if it was in my own death—seemed hotter than any flame I could produce.

But he didn't need to know, and since my time was coming to a close, he didn't have to. I could flit in and out of his long life and be no more than a blip. Yes. I could do that. I could love him to distraction, lose myself in the beautiful newness of a fleeting love, and no one would be the wiser. Especially him. It would be the one gift I could give myself—a single bit of happiness in a rather difficult and awful life.

I wasn't as limited as I'd let everyone believe. Sure, I'm blind in the most basic of senses, but the beauty of being an Oracle is it didn't matter. I saw so much more with my mind; I didn't *need* my eyes. But he came after my visions dried up, and of all the things I saw, of all the events I foretold...

I didn't see him. And I should have.

Maybe if I'd have seen him, I would have done things differently.

NICOLA—AFTER

The darkness blanketing me didn't seem safe. There were things lurking here, evil things, horrible things. Things who whispered in my ear about murder and blood and death. They told me horrific tales of slain children and bloodied sacrifices and ripping the very fabric of the afterlife to shreds.

I wanted out of this darkness—out of the blackness and thick, oily dank of the hell imprisoning me. I was scared—lost and detached from reality and my body, and all I wanted was to make it to the light.

I clawed and scratched and screamed, but I couldn't find a way out of the darkness. In the back of my mind, I knew I belonged here. I knew I deserved this prison. I couldn't remember what I'd done, but I knew... I knew it was a price I had to pay.

And I paid—minute after minute, day after day, month after month—until time lost its meaning and I fell asleep in the cold darkness of my own hell.

I

NICOLA—AFTER

I COME BACK TO MYSELF SLOWLY——PAINFULLY——IN FITS AND starts of consciousness. Feeling my heart first, the slow plodding of a body in rest, then the cool stagnant air of a closed room on my skin. The rough but soft bedding surrounding my legs and then the thing that makes my eyes flash open in fear——the warm heat of a hand on mine. I sit up as if I was shot from a cannon, my eyes flashing open for the first time in what feels like a long time.

I can't remember what I'm so afraid of...

My mind trills with the alarm of danger, but I can't place where it's coming from or why. As my eyes scan the dim room, they instantly snag on the form of a man standing next to me. His body is enormous, standing several inches over six feet, his legs encased in dark denim and feet shod in dangerous black boots. His hair, which is trapped beneath the raised hood of his sweater, is not quite black but close enough to be confused for it, matching the thick but groomed beard decorating his jaw. His eyes, which are locked on me, are the color of a decadent milk chocolate. His hands reach for me, and my first feeling is fear—dark and clawing— and I rear back, pressing myself into the pillows of the narrow bed I'm sitting on.

Vaguely, my mind latches onto the fact that this is a hospital, but I'm not sure if I'm right or if this is a dream or if I really am in the danger my heart and mind are screaming at me I'm in.

"Nicola, sweetheart, it's okay. You're in the hospital, baby," his rough voice says soothingly, but I am not soothed. I am nowhere near the realm of soothed. It doesn't matter that this forbidding man has a voice that calls to me. The name he called me doesn't sound right, for one, and as handsome as this man is, I have no idea who he is supposed to be to me. He has to be in the wrong room, right?

Right?

He grabs my hand, gently closing his large fingers

over mine, and although the heat of him is nice—almost calming—I don't want this stranger touching me. I don't want him looking at me like this—the wary hesitance on his bearded face is twisting my stomach in knots and the name he called me...

That's not me. That's not my name.

"Th-that's not my name," I tell him as I shake my head. He has it wrong. The wrong room or wrong woman or something. His face is wrong, his expression is hurt mixed with longing and something worse—fear.

Wrong, wrong, wrong.

"What is your name then?" he asks, his voice calm and controlled as he presses the square orange button on the bedrail. I follow the motion of his hand as he stabs the button, trying to think...

"It's... Well..." I pause, concentrating on a fact which should be so easy to remember, but all I come up with is... *nothing.*

"I-I don't know," I stutter frowning at the white coverlet warming my legs.

I want to say I was holding it together. I want to say my brain went right to denial—which would have helped the situation vastly—that I didn't feel a burning ache in my chest from fear and uncertainty, and Fates knew what else.

But I do—I do feel the ache of loss, of confusion, of unbridled fear.

I don't know my name. How can I not know my name? And who is he? Why is he looking at me like this? What happened to me?

I feel the burn of my breaths coming too fast and my heart pounding too hard. The room begins to spin.

I can't get air… No air… I don't want to go back to the darkness. Nononononononononononono…

The man starts yelling—first at me to breathe and then at the closed door, roaring for help. But his voice is fading, and the room's lights dim further, my sight tunneling to pinpoints. For the life of me, I can't figure out why the fact I'm seeing the light sticks in my mind just before I pass out.

I COME TO WITH MUCH LESS FANFARE THAN THE LAST TIME. The man isn't there, but a tall, auburn-haired woman is folded in the bedside chair, her eyes closed and her breaths coming in the deep pulls of sleep. Her head is at such an odd angle, resting on her bent, scrub-covered knees as she sleeps curled into an awkward ball in the seat.

I don't want to wake her, but there are a few issues I need to worry about. First, I seem to be attached to this bed by a thick padded cuff on each wrist. This is concerning on so many levels, I'm not sure my brain is taking the time to process it. Second, the original problem of not knowing who I am or where I am or why I'm here is still an issue. A major one. I hate not knowing myself, I hate not knowing how I got here. I clear my throat, realizing too late that at some point I must have been screaming because my throat is on fire.

What the hell happened to me?

The woman comes awake with a start, jumping from her curled ball to her feet with a preternatural grace, her eyes flashing a phosphorescent green. It should worry me. It really should, but for some reason, it doesn't.

"You're not human," I hoarsely croak, stating the obvious. Her lips stretch into a sardonic smile, and it takes her beauty up about ten notches. Her large, almost feline eyes have faded to an odd shade of amber, framed by thick, dark lashes, and she doesn't have a stitch of makeup on her face.

"Neither are you," she returns, her voice a husky alto. This information is not shocking—just like her fantastical jump to her feet, I am not moved. I must have known this before.

Before, I internally scoff. I already hate the word, but I think I need to know a bit more about this 'before' because my brain is not supplying anything other than an extreme lack of shock.

"Are you a healer?" I ask on a wince. What the hell happened to my voice? The woman nods as she pours water into a small blue plastic cup on a rolling bedside table. She eyes my wrists for a moment and plops the pitcher back on the surface with an indelicate thunk.

"My name is Willa, I'm your physician. If I remove your restraints, do you promise not to harm yourself?" she asks with a raised eyebrow. Her eyebrow tells me my answer better be yes, and then her question finally starts to make sense in my head.

I hurt myself? On purpose?

I feel my eyes widen in the surprise I should have had for her jump or her non-human statement, and I quickly nod. Her swift, efficient fingers have my wrists free in mere seconds, but better, her voice prattles on with information. Any and all information is helpful at this point.

"I removed your Foley after your first wake-up call," she says as she moves from my wrists to wave a penlight in front of my eyes. "You've been here for about four months. We weren't sure if you'd ever wake up. Normally, someone of your species should have been up and about ages ago—a week at most, but you're not healing as fast as you should."

Her statement stops me. *I have no idea what I am.*

"Species?" I ask.

"You have no idea, do you?"

"I don't even know my own name, so no, I have absolutely no fucking idea what's going on. Care to share with the class?" I snap. I don't want to snap at her, but I just want to know all of the shit I don't know already.

"Snarky. I like it. I can work with snark, just no more screaming, mmm-kay?"

So this explains what happened to my throat.

"Deal," I reply and Willa holds out the cup as I take a healthy swig. The cool water hits my throat, easing the burn.

"Your name is Nicola. The man who was here before? His name is Kyle. He's your husband."

"Don't start off small, Willa. *Jesus,*" a rumbling voice sounds from the doorway.

The man—Kyle—is in the same clothes as the last time, but his hood has been lowered, giving him a slightly less sinister quality and he now has a pair of thick-framed glasses perched on his nose. His hair is a rumpled mess, as if he has run his hands through it, slept on it, electrocuted himself and possibly took a stroll through a hurricane. He is haggard—probably hasn't slept at all in who knows how long, and immediately I want to give him a hug, make him some food and offer the bed to him so he can get some damn rest.

I want to be freaked at the husband comment Willa threw out there like it was no big deal, but I don't think I can be. *Why else would he be here? Why else would he come back? And why do I want to comfort him?*

"Of all the information I need to know, a husband would be at the top of the list, don't you think?" I retort with a shrug.

"You aren't surprised?" Kyle asks.

"I'm finding very few things have surprised me thus far. Can you come in and take a load off? You look like you've been put through the wringer twice."

I get a scowl, a grunted affirmative and a slow shuffle-walk to the bedside chair Willa vacated. In my bones, I know the shuffle is a ruse. He's moving slowly on purpose so I won't freak out. Standing, he has to be closer to seven feet than to six, but I can tell his height and the considerable bulk to his muscles do not hinder his speed in the slightest.

"While all this is well and good, you still haven't told me how I got here or what I am." The question leaves my mouth without thought, and when they exchange a wary glance, I'm not sure I want to know anymore.

NICOLA—NEW ENGLAND 1723

I ran as fast as my little feet could carry me through the brush, stumbling to my hands and knees more times than I could count. Every single day I breathed, I cursed my visions and my sightless eyes, but on days like today, I wished for death more and more.

If I could die—which it seemed I couldn't—I hoped it would be painless, but I had seen death over and over again, and I knew better. Branches whipped my cheeks, stones gouged my feet, but still I ran. Those switches were nothing compared to the danger behind me. He was coming, and he would do horrible things to me when I wouldn't tell him what was to pass.

Didn't he know? I only told death stories, and if death was not to pass, I couldn't tell anyone anything. He'd tried cutting the visions out of me, tried breaking my bones, starving me—but I couldn't tell him what I didn't know.

At first, he called me a devil. Told me I was made of fire and I would bring him death. I'd been drawn to the woman I saw in my vision—not him. She was dying very soon, bound and shackled in a horrific prison where her breaths became more and more labored and her broken body had to fight minute by minute just to keep going. I knew if I were near, she could return to the sky—I could help this good woman start again. I remembered the rites my mother said when papa passed, they were the only good things I remembered about her since she abandoned me in this new place to survive on my own. Every time I saw a good soul die in my visions, I would try to help them move on.

He'd caught me freeing the woman—her body already gone, but her soul was safe now that I'd saved it. He saw my wings, my fire and told me I was of the fallen. When he realized my blindness, he called me Oracle—he said I could tell him his future.

I couldn't. I could only tell him death.

And then the torture started. He must not have had manacles small enough for my eight-year-old wrists—or maybe he did but once he'd starved me for a month, my already thin wrists were able to slip from the irons and I was free.

But not if he caught me.

I felt the air change, the rush of water met my ears just before the fresh, salty smell of the ocean hit my nose. I ran faster until the ground seemed to dip beneath my feet. I tripped again, sliding at breakneck speeds through the rocks toward the sound of crashing waves.

But then cool, slender hands caught me. They weren't his hands—this I knew.

"Do not worry, child. I have come to help you," a woman's voice crooned as she hugged me to her chest. Her accent was Irish and as soft as a cool summer breeze.

The sound of the man's thrashing through the forest filtered through the trees, and I curled into her, frightened. I didn't want any more of his knives or fists. I didn't want his hot, putrid breath on my face as he called me devil, abomination, demon, harlot. I didn't know what harlot meant, but from his tone, I knew it was bad. I wasn't bad. I was a good girl. I knew I wasn't human, but I couldn't help that. I was born to my strangeness just as I'd been born without sight.

"Cover your ears, child, and I'll take care of this filth," she instructed, calmly brushing my matted hair back from my face. I knew she was going to kill him, and I knew killing was bad, but she was saving me. I couldn't find it in me to care for the man who had tortured me and so many others.

"Wait!" I cried as I clutched to her willowy arm. I didn't want her to leave me. What if she didn't succeed? I needed to have a little piece of her.

"Yes, dearie?" she answered, her voice like watered silk.

"What is your name? I never knew his name. I want to know your name," my voice broke—I was so close to breaking myself.

"My name is Iva, dearie, and I've been looking for you."

2

KYLE—BEFORE

THERE ARE QUITE A FEW THINGS I'D FOUND FOR OTHER FOLKS over the years. Lost people, stolen objects, fugitives on the run from the King. It didn't matter how far or how long they ran, I always found them. I was good at my job, working closely with the King—and West when necessary—but also with other members of the Ethereal. Witches, Warlocks, Shapeshifters—it was known far and wide if you wanted someone or something found, you came to me.

But I had scruples. The people who came to me knew my code. I didn't find anything if I didn't know the story behind it. There had to be a damn good reason I went looking for someone. There had been several times over the years where the story I'd been told was nowhere near the truth. An abusive husband looking for his wife and children, a thief wanting me to do his dirty work, a corrupt leader looking for a whistleblower...

Life didn't quite work out so well for those men.

I had plenty of business—enough where I could pick and choose my jobs based on what interested me—and despite the periphery I consistently found myself on, I felt included with my species. So, when my King called me, I came without question.

I never did get to find out why he needed me.

Too much happened. Nicola happened.

I'll never forget the first time I saw her. If I hadn't been the one to open the door that day, who knows what would have happened. But I was. I saw her. I heard her and knew she was mine.

Maybe if I'd never heard her voice—if I hadn't let her flash of brilliant red hair catch my eye—I could have saved us both.

POUNDING CAME FROM THE SOLID OAK FRONT DOOR OF THE Grand Lake cabin. The pounding was proceeded by five, incessant doorbell rings. Both of these actions were completely unnecessary. Visitors were more than just announced—before you could access the property, you had to pass through an eight-foot wrought-iron security gate complete with digital surveillance. To gain entry without someone in this house knowing, you needed either a remote or thumbprint access. The person on the other side of this door had neither. Not to mention, Ian brought her here, and as far as I knew, he was still parking the car. Why she couldn't drive herself, I didn't know.

At first, I had no idea she was blind. I had no idea who she was at all. All I knew was John asked me to greet our guest, and if his tone was derisive to the point of scathing, well, it wasn't my place to judge.

The woman standing at the threshold was a tiny slip of a thing, but at six-foot-seven, everyone is tiny compared to me. She topped out at a respectable five-five with wildly curly, deep red hair and large, cornflower blue eyes that didn't quite meet mine. Her dewy, porcelain skin was flawless without a single stitch of makeup, and I was immediately transfixed by the delicate rose color of her full lips. My eyes took a trip over her body. Her outfit—a royal blue, spaghetti strapped dress under a waspish cardigan—was paired with simple tan flats and hid exactly zero of her curves. Generous bosom, tiny waist, hips and thighs that could make a man weep and short but slim legs. I immediately chided myself for giving her a full head-to-toe and brought my eyes back up to her face. She wore no jewelry, no makeup, and the bulk of her curly hair was wild except for two braids at each temple that pulled a bit of it back from her face. Her lips parted to speak, and my eyes became laser-focused on her plump lower lip.

It wasn't until Ian stomped up the steps behind her did I realize I was just standing there staring, etching each of her features into my brain.

"You couldn't wait the three minutes for me to park the car? Seriously, Nicola?" Ian grumbled. He paused and waited for me, but I was still stuck on her face. "You just going to stand there, man? You're letting all the bought air out," he chided, nudging past the woman—Nicola—and throwing a shoulder into my arm, snapping me out of it.

I stepped back, sweeping my hand wide for her to enter. After a beat of her remaining immobile, I said, "Any day now, sweetheart."

All I got was a scathing raised eyebrow in response. Then, I noticed the white, probing cane in her hand and immediately felt like a first-rate jackass. Well, this explained why she didn't drive herself.

"Your hospitality is impeccable," Nicola said, her

faint British accent curling the sarcasm into a less-than-biting comeback. Maybe it was her accent or the husky rasp of her voice or her unearthly beauty, but I was mesmerized. I immediately felt the hit to my man card that the word 'mesmerized' was even in my vocabulary, but the urge to curl around her, to touch her pale, creamy skin, to protect her—to keep her close to me - rose in me faster than I could help.

I want to say I was calm and collected, but I'd be lying. My only saving grace was her blindness. Otherwise, she would've seen my phase, my fangs, my talons, the problematic bulge in my jeans. How lucky was I no one saw my trip into crazy town?

"Is there some reason you have phased, Wraith? Should I worry for my safety or are you going to play nice?" she challenged, alerting me to the fact her blindness did not detract in any way from her perceptiveness. Shit.

"How did you know?" I asked around my fangs, my voice a garbled mess.

"Phoenixes naturally have a keen sense of hearing. My blindness dials that up to eleven. I heard your talons grow, the bones in your face crack, and the infinitesimal flick of your eyes bleeding to black. Now, are you planning on killing me or offering your arm so I don't bang my shin on every stick of furniture in this house trying to find John?"

"I won't hurt you, Shortcake. You just quoted Spinal Tap. That means we have to be friends now."

"Not if you keep calling me Shortcake. Think of something original, will you, or else I might just start calling you Sasquatch," she returned, but our banter was interrupted by a crash of a dish breaking in the kitchen.

I grabbed her without thought, sweeping her up into my arms and striding through the great room to the source of the sound. Honestly, I was afraid for John. His health wasn't what it should be, his hair was turning gray faster and faster, and Olivia was nowhere to be found. He had yet to tell me why he'd called on me, and with each passing day here holed up in this house while our people—our families—were exterminated... the pit in my stomach grew larger and larger.

My hackles were up already, a ripple of unease flashing across my skin as I crossed the threshold of the kitchen to see Evangeline tackle Rhys to the ground before he could reach for Aurelia.

Aurelia and Rhys came to us days ago after a nasty situation at Aurelia's art show in Denver. Evidently, Phoenixes weren't just exterminating Wraiths—they were taking out any and all threats to the Primary, the

Phoenixes' leader. Why Aurelia was considered a threat, I had no idea, but if she needed the help, I'd be happy to give it to her. Granted, she didn't need much help. She'd handed me my ass yesterday in the training room without breaking a sweat. I was really trying there at the end and she whooped my ass without even trying.

But right now, she didn't look like she could do anything to help herself. She stood clutching the granite of the center island, the force of her grip cracking the stone as her body bowed in agony. I lowered Nicola to her feet, setting her to my right as we watched Evan try to keep Rhys from reaching his woman.

"Don't touch her! Her Aegis will kill you!" Evangeline shouted in his face, just as John traveled in next to me, with Aidan, Cam, Asher, West and Ian bringing up the rear.

"Aegis? She's a fucking Aegis, and you didn't tell me? Why?" Rhys roared, understandably upset.

I'd heard of the Aegis, a type of Phoenix whose main ability manifested itself into an electrical shield, but no more than whispers, and I sure as shit had never seen an adult one. As far as I knew no one had because young Aegis could not control their abilities—usually ending up blowing themselves to smithereens.

"Because I told her not to," John answered, his voice threaded with a tired exasperation.

"And why's that, John? What reason could you possibly have for not telling me my mate is a fucking time bomb?"

"Because the Primary would have seen," Nicola piped in, her lilting voice a husky whisper in the middle of the rage-fueled room.

"And who the fuck are you?" Rhys snarled as he picked himself up off the floor, his eyes flitting to each person before landing on her.

"My name is Nicola, and I am the Primary's second," she said as she gave him a dainty bow.

"You!" he growled as his confusion turned into recognition, and I didn't think—I just acted. Rhys lunged for Nicola, but before he could close the last few inches, I pulled her behind me and put a fist to his temple.

My phase was instantaneous as I placed my body between the threat and her. I didn't quite understand what the hell was happening to me—why I wanted to protect her with all of me—I just knew this fucker wasn't touching her. Not on my watch.

He took a minute to shake off my hit, and I just knew he was debating on putting a bullet in me, but Fuck. That. He wasn't getting to her. No fucking way.

Then her hand was on my shoulder. I knew it was her—it had to be. I'd never felt the chord of tension in me ease before—the one that curled in my gut, kept me searching for the one thing I'd never found. Tendrils of peace mixed with want and an urge to slice my fangs into the column of her throat hit me all at once, jarring me. My phase bled from me, but I knew the danger wasn't over. I couldn't deal with all of these issues at once—I needed to handle this shit first.

Rhys relaxed, but his hand twitched just the wrong way. He seemed like a good enough guy, but I knew the lengths he would go to protect Aurelia. I knew better now in the five minutes I'd been in Nicola's presence than I ever did before. So when his finger moved, edging toward the Ruger I knew was in his spine holster, I took him to the ground.

No one was getting to her. No matter what.

KYLE—AFTER

I don't trust her. Or this. Any of this. I'd seen her when Iva was squatting like a toad inside her body, and I wasn't sure if I could ever trust her again. Why did she let him do this to her? Didn't she figure it out already? Devereux was never going to let me live. It didn't matter what he promised her—Devereux Emerson was the worst sort of man. Soulless.

If she'd never have said yes to him, at least my

sacrifice would have been for something. But she thought I needed saving, and when Nicola Miller thinks someone needs saving, she will sacrifice everything, move heaven and earth to make sure they stay saved. If Aurelia and Mena had even an inkling of what she'd done—what she'd lived through—to keep them alive...

To keep me alive.

And she could remember none of it. Not them, not me, not even her own fucking name. But she wanted to know what happened, and it felt wrong not to tell her. I met her odd amber eyes. I missed her old ones. I missed the old Nicola.

"Look, Nic," I broke off. She flinched every time I said her name. Fine. "Alright, no saying that name, huh?" I ask trying to keep a lid on the surge of anger ready to erupt.

"It feels wrong. Like I'd been called something else," Nicola confesses, staring at her knees instead of looking me in the eye.

"You mean like Iva?" I spit, the anger cresting and spilling over and out of my mouth. As soon as the name passes my lips I regret it. Her already pale face goes a startling shade of gray, and she curls into herself, flinching back from me.

"Do-don't say that name. Th-that's a bad name," she shudders, covering her face with her hands.

I pull myself up and out of my seat, curling myself around her—doing my best to protect her from the aftermath of my words, feeling like the worst sort of prick. I knew what she'd lived through. I knew, and I still sliced at her with my fucking tongue. Fuck.

"I'm sorry, Shortcake. I won't say it again. I'm sorry, baby," I murmur as I put my arms around her and try to gently pull her hands from her face. Giving up when I meet solid resistance, I scoop her up, trading places and settling her cradled in my lap. I didn't realize how much weight she'd lost lying immobile on this bed for months, but she feels too light in my arms. Too light, too fragile, and I hate this for her.

My strong mate suffered no fools. Her blindness did not debilitate her in any way, and her tongue was wielded like a weapon.

I glance up to see Willa giving me a look that tells me if we weren't on ground warded against violence, she would have kicked my ass up and down this hospital.

Get your head out of your ass, she mouths at me and stalks out of the room, but remembering herself at the last second and stops the door before it slams. The quiet snick of the latch the only sound in the room except for Nicola's shuddered breathing.

"Shh, Shortcake. You're alright, you'll be alright," I

murmur as I rock her back and forth to try and soothe her.

"That has to be the worst nickname ever. Think of something else, please," she croaks into my chest, and I cannot help my roar of laughter.

Maybe she's my Nic after all.

3

NICOLA—AFTER

His deep, booming laugh scares the crap out of me at first—I didn't think I'd said anything funny—but the longer he laughs, the more I can't help the giggle that slips out of my mouth. His outburst shaves the worry from him, and his scowl has left the building. It completely transforms his face, it makes me notice how full his lips are, how young he looks when he isn't constantly frowning, scowling or brooding.

"Some things never change," Kyle says chuckling, giving me a little squeeze.

"What do you mean?" I ask, enjoying the thick weight of his arms around me. I don't know exactly when cuddling became our thing, but I prefer it to the standoffishness of earlier. His arms feel wonderful, and I had no idea I was missing them until just this moment.

"You hated the nickname before, too. It's good to see something staying the same is all."

The statement stings. It reminds me I am a shell of the woman he knew, a withered husk of a woman. I don't even know my last name. *How awful is that?*

But then I realize if some things are the same, then maybe I could get my memories back. *Maybe I could get my life back.*

"So you're my husband, huh?" I question as I lay my head back down on his shoulder and am immediately hit with how good he smells. It isn't cologne, but rather the natural scent of citrus and man. I have to fight the urge to stick my nose in his neck and breathe him in.

"Not the way humans see it, but in the way of my people, yes, I'm your husband," he replies.

"Are your people not my people?" I ask because he piqued my interest. Were we not the same?

"We aren't the same species, but it is becoming more common for inter-species unions. It's not frowned upon or anything, just not common."

Well, at least there was that. I'd hate it if people judged us just based on who we chose as a partner. It seems silly to hate someone based solely on whom they choose to love.

"What are you?" I ask. I want to know as much as I could about this man I had forgotten.

"Species or profession?" he rumbles, his voice wary.

"All of the above."

"Professionally, I am a Tracker. Humans would liken it to a bounty hunter, but I can find just about anything—objects included. Species... I am a Wraith. I consume deserving souls to ferry them to hell," he informs me, his voice and body tense.

Something tells me this isn't everything, but I can't put my finger on it. When his body practically vibrates with tension, I meet his eyes.

Whoa. Did Kyle think I would judge him? His seemed a noble profession and purpose. Bringing my hand up to rest on his chest, I tried to tame the wary beast in him. His muscles relaxed a fraction.

"And I am?" I continue, his muscles tensing once again. Am I something bad?

"Species or profession?" he asks again, his body vibrating.

"All of the above," I repeat on a whisper.

"Species, you are a Phoenix. You help deserving souls move on to be reborn." Holy shit. *I was cool.*

"And professionally?" I ask because although he had told me something good—at least I thought it was good—he is strung tighter than a bow.

"You... you used to be an Oracle, but I don't know if this is something you can still be," he finishes, his voice lowering to a whisper.

"Why?" I ask even though I don't want to.

"You're not blind anymore," he murmurs and then I get why he was so tense. This was the bad. Something happened to me. I was changed somehow. A jagged feeling of dread fills me, and I don't want to ask, but I have to.

"It's bad I'm not blind anymore, isn't it? It isn't like I was healed or anything. Something bad happened to me," I murmur. I knew in my gut it was worse than whatever I could manage to cook up in my head. I was in a hospital, for fuck's sake. It had to be bad.

"Yeah, baby," he whispers, his voice broken. Did something happen to him? Was he hurt? I may be the only one without a memory, but he knew what happened. He knew, and it made it worse.

"Did it happen to you, too?" I ask, tears clogging my already sore throat. I didn't want this for him. I didn't want him hurt or scared or unsafe.

"Not exactly, but we both endured some bad shit. You just got the worst of it," he answers, his arms squeezing me tighter.

At that moment I was glad I got the worst. I'd take

anything if it meant he didn't get the short end of the stick, too. But I also didn't think I could take more.

"I don't... I don't think I can know all of it right now. I don't think I can handle it. I feel... *raw.*"

"Anytime you want to know, whatever you want to know, just ask."

I didn't know if I would ever get the courage to ask him what happened.

Maybe it was better not knowing.

NICOLA—OREGON 1855

The guilt clawed at me. I knew exactly what would happen. Of course, I did. I knew it as much as I knew my own name. Aurelia Constantine wouldn't heed my warning—she wouldn't leave when I told her to, she wouldn't take the precautions I warned her about. Aurelia would think she had all the time in the world. She would think my warning was nonsense. She wouldn't hold her love close to her, realize I was right and leave her cold mother, her secretive twin, and neglectful father to their own fate as she made her life anew.

No.

She would endure the worst things... torture, pain, loss, death—all because I couldn't make myself clear enough. I couldn't see her with my eyes, but I knew every expression of her face and every silent gesture of her hands and set to her shoulders.

I'd seen them—maybe not with my eyes, but definitely with my mind. I'd seen the luminescent caramel skin of her cheek as her lips twisted in a wry smile and the delicate slope of her neck as she shrugged in indecision. The incandescent light in her eyes which told everyone what she was...

My power had grown more than I ever thought possible in the last century, but the slip of the woman before me? She would surpass me one day—I knew it. So I had to keep her safe from Iva—I had to change her fate. I had to get her out of here one way or another. There were things I couldn't tell her—things if she knew would alter her course. Things that would give me away as well.

My vagueness would cost Aurelia dearly, and I couldn't figure out how to change it. When she left, hot tears fell from my sightless eyes as I stifled my sobs in my fist. I couldn't let the Soldiers know of my pain.

Soldiers.

Might as well call them what they were—jailers. I was as much a prisoner here as I was a leader. Every single step, every decision, every word that passed my lips was watched and cataloged and reported to Iva. The woman who was so long ago my savior was now my warden.

I had to dry my tears, I couldn't let anyone know.

I had to figure out a way to save them—if it was the last thing I did.

HIS SCREAMS REACHED MY EARS LONG BEFORE I MADE IT through the door. I had no idea a man could make that sound, let alone survive what was causing it. Rhys was paying a price I could not afford to pay—he stopped an evil before it could come to pass, and for this, I would always be grateful. He may well have saved us all with his sacrifice.

Julian was Iva's most trusted Soldier. He took the messier and most dubious of jobs. Nothing was off limits for him. He did things even I didn't know about—things I didn't want to know about. He thirsted for it—his necessity to hunt and kill became an aura around him even I could see. There was nothing left of the man he was before Iva got her hooks into him.

Rhys sent Julian to his death—his own brother—because Julian refused to deny our leader and set out to assassinate the Wraith Queen. In a way, I felt complicit in Julian's death and Rhys' torture. I saw it days ago, long before Rhys made the decision himself. I saw Julian's death and his well-deserved trip to hell.

Rhys' screams hit me in the gut again and again. I had to keep my face stony, but inside I was dying—dying for this man and what I would have to do to him. I used my senses to navigate my way to the ceremonial chamber. That's what Iva called it. In my head, I called it what it was—a bloody torture chamber. Ceremony. No one in their right mind would call this anything but torture.

My ears rang from the roar of agony coming from Rhys' mouth. The smell of burnt flesh hit my nose, and I held back a gag by the skin of my teeth. Phoenixes usually couldn't be burned—but if someone were to heat a Morganite blade and press it to our skin... I couldn't hold back the shudder of sympathy pain for Rhys. This was going too far, I had to figure out a way to stop this before she killed him.

"I detest the smell of burning flesh, Iva-dear. Could you desist, please? It is turning my stomach," I complained, my voice laced with a touch of sullen irritation to hide my revulsion.

"I would, but this wee child needs to answer my question first," she purred.

"And what question might that be? Honestly, Iva.

Must you resort to burning? It will be weeks before I can eat meat again," I scolded in a bored tone. It's possible I may never eat anything ever again after this.

"I want him to accept the binding, and he is refusing to obey his Primary. He's being a naughty, naughty boy," she cooed.

"Be that as it may, dear, torture only works until your plaything is dead and your toy is close to the veil. Might I give it a go?"

I need to give this man a break. I have to get her away from him and get this hell to stop.

"You think you can break him? He's been here for a week and nothing. You think you have it in you?" she taunted, a smile in her voice knowing I have a strict aversion to torture. Given my past, you'd think she'd be mindful of it, but not Iva. It doesn't really matter how blank my face is or how bored my tone is. She'll still needle me.

"Maybe I don't need to torture him to get him to do what I want. Give me the room, and if I cannot turn his mind, you can continue burning him until you get the outcome you desire," I offered.

I don't see her nod, but I feel her acquiescence.

"Fine, you have one hour. But if you fail, you'll watch me burn him," she tossed back as I heard her voice carry from the room. A few Soldiers stayed put until I shooed them from the room. Only when the room was cleared did I breathe a sigh of relief.

I made my way closer to Rhys, his pained, labored breathing calling to me. He reminded me of the poor woman I'd sent on so long ago as a child. She'd been burned too, and the smell brought back all the pain I'd felt her endure at the hands of a wayward Puritan.

"Rhys?" I whispered and got a grunt in response.

"I don't have much time, but I need your help. You have to live, darling boy. For Aurelia's sake, you have to live. I can't make you take the binding, but if you do, I can stop this torture and maybe—just maybe—save your love's life. I know if I do not bind the two of you, she will die, Rhys, and it will be soon. With what Iva has planned for her, death will not be a relief. I need your help. Will you help me?" I begged.

"S-she'll die? True death?" he croaked.

"Yes. And Iva will not send her on. She'll use her as an example. Her soul will be trapped here."

"Y-you know this? For certain?"

"Yes. Unless you bind her," I swore. I wasn't lying—this wasn't a ploy to change Rhys' mind. Aurelia Constantine's death had run over and over in my mind. Nothing else I'd done had changed it. My vague warning did nothing—my talks with Iva did nothing. This was my last chance to change it.

"Then do it. I accept," Rhys murmured.

By the time Iva came back, his and Aurelia's binding was complete with a minor change I hope one day they'd forgive me for.

"Do I get to burn him then?" she asked as she bustled into the room along with her guards.

"Afraid not, Iva-dear. The binding is complete with a nice little addition I think you'll appreciate," I replied.

"Oh?"

"Oh, yes," I purred, praying my voice didn't betray me. "I made it a dual bond. What happens to one, happens to both. He won't be able to nick himself shaving without her bleeding. I thought you'd like that."

Bragging was the only way prove myself to Iva. It was the only way my plan would even have a chance at working.

"Brava, dearie. I wish I'd thought it up."

"You bitch!" Rhys railed, not realizing I was warning him as much as I was proving my allegiance once more.

"Now, now. Don't be cross, Rhys. There's no changing it now," I scolded him, and it was true.

Their path together was now set in stone.

4

KYLE—AFTER

SOMEHOW, BOTH NICOLA AND I FELL ASLEEP ON THE TINY AS shit torture chamber called a hospital bed. I'm taking up the majority of the bed, and Nicola is tucked into my side, her fiery red hair spread across my chest, her soft snuffling breaths the only sound in the room. It isn't the first time I've woken up this way, and I'd missed it. This is what I'd been dreaming about for months, her warm little body next to mine. It's what got me through the cold nights trapped in my filthy cell in the Emerson's dungeon.

The memory of her pales to reality. I forgot the way her skin smells, the natural cinnamon scent mixed with woman. I forgot how hot her body is when she's sleeping, as if her body temperature notches up ten degrees as soon as her eyelids close. I missed her warmth. Without her in my arms, I've felt colder than I'd ever felt before in my life, even when I'd been tracking down a murderer in the Canadian Rockies. Alberta is not my favorite place to be in the dead of winter, I don't give a shit how good the skiing is.

I damn near lost a toe on that hunt.

But I didn't know what warmth was until I held her all night long. I didn't know how much I would miss it when her heat was gone. Now that I have it back… I don't know what I'd do if I'd lost it again.

Especially now.

Nicola's delicate hand rests on my left pec, just over my heart, and if I could, I'd draw her spot against my body with permanent marker. This is exactly where her body goes—this is the exact spot she used to take. I don't know if I put her here or if she migrated here on her own, but I don't want this to end. I don't want her to wake up without knowing us or me again.

But I know she will. Because the Nicola I knew is gone—maybe forever.

I cover her hand with mine, and I get to enjoy a few moments of my peace before her hand startles under mine. As I look down into her amber eyes, I hate that I wish they were blue.

KYLE—BEFORE

I took her to my safe place—no one knew about the house tucked in the dense forest of the Appalachians foothills of Kentucky. Purchased over seven decades ago under a false name, I suppose the only people who knew about the property were me and the United States government, but this isolated cabin had probably been long forgotten by any humans who'd dealt with it. Most of them were likely dead or in retirement homes by now.

In a location populated sparsely by one-room hunting cabins, my house was on the large side. A single story ranch-style home with a deep wrap-around porch, it was built by my own two hands and retrofitted to accommodate my size. I was proud of every single board, nail, and brick.

I came here often in between hunts to decompress —needing the solitude and isolation so I wouldn't go crazy. I dealt with a bevy of unsavory characters in my line of work, and I needed time to myself so I wouldn't turn into a feral, heart-eating monster. If you were taunted with your favorite steak, you could only smell the meat for so long before pouncing. This cabin kept me away from the scent—away from the knife edge of losing my mind.

I studied the exterior with fresh eyes and wished fervently that she could see it like I could. The tin roof gleamed in spots where the sun filtered in through the trees. The porch, stained a rich cherry, contrasted with the gray-green paint. Each of the planks were in good repair and freshly sealed against the summer rains.

I held Nicola's warm body to me as my feet met the dirt. I'd made sure no one could travel directly into my house, and the grounds were filled with traps to keep unwanted persons away. Given my line of work, I couldn't be too careful.

"The house is warded," Nicola murmured as soon as her feet touched the ground. Her eyes never trailed from my chest. I'd give her shit for it, but I know she's not really looking at me. It took me about three seconds to adjust to her process. I can't call it a limitation or a handicap—because she isn't handicapped and doesn't have many limitations—but her method of doing things is a little different than someone who can see twenty-twenty.

"How do you know?" I asked. I don't know why I didn't think of her being able to tell the house was warded. She had proven to be much more perceptive than a sighted person.

"I feel it. It's like a buzzing against my skin. Quite unpleasant," she said as she rubbed her hands over her arms as if she were cold. It didn't matter it was July in Kentucky and likely well over ninety degrees, she felt the full-tilt chill warning her to stay away.

"It should go away once we get inside," I assured her as I grabbed her hand to lead her inside, but she tugged at my hand.

"You said no one knew about this place. How did you get it warded?" she asked, her face confused.

"Promise not to tell?" I didn't think I'd have to get into my lineage just yet. Fuck.

"I have no one to tell, so, absolutely," she replied with a delicate shrug.

"I did it," I admitted.

"I was unaware Wraiths possessed that ability."

"They don't," I muttered under my breath as I pulled her through the ward and up the porch steps, unlocking the front door.

With my first steps inside, I felt the weight of worry fall off of me. No one could get into this house, and no one could come within five hundred meters of it without me knowing. I led her through the main room —a great room filled with comfy furniture and a television which took up about eighty percent of the eastern wall—and headed toward the kitchen. I led her to a barstool which butted up against the kitchen island and settled in for the inquisition.

"You're not all Wraith, are you?" Nicola murmured, more to herself than to ask me.

"Nope," I answered as I put the island between us, grabbed a beer from the fridge, popped the top with the bottle opener installed in the counter face, and took a deep pull. I didn't need this woman to judge my lineage and if she did—I'd know the attraction I felt for her was off. It had to be, right? Wraiths and Phoenixes didn't mix. Hell, half of my friends were dead because of a Phoenix. I should hate them.

"So loquacious. Sore subject?" Nicola asked, her head tilting in sympathy. Something told me Nicola was no stranger to the oddities of the Ethereal. There was no judgment in her voice, no censure. She either didn't mind it or really didn't give a shit about the major sticking point so many did. Growing up, my oddities made for few friends and a bevy of enemies.

And she didn't give a single fuck.

"It isn't something I talk about. My mother was a Witch. My father was a Wraith. They were bonded, and she died when I was a boy, taking my father with her when she went. I lived with my grandmama—my mama's mother—until I was old enough to be on my own."

"I bet your grandmother taught you everything

there was to know about spells, didn't she?" she asked with a slight laugh in her voice.

"She taught me enough to be dangerous—more to myself than to anyone else," I said as I plunked my beer on the counter, rounded the island and invaded her space. Swiveling the barstool so I stood between her legs.

"You don't care, do you?" I asked as I cupped her chin in my palm, staring into those beautiful blues, watching as her face turned from surprise to anger in a flash.

"Of course not! No one can decide the circumstances of their birth. Blaming someone for their lineage is... is... utter *bullshit*," she spat, the curse word sounding hilarious coming out of her mouth.

I couldn't help myself—I swear I couldn't. Nothing could have stopped me from kissing that frown right off her face. Nothing else she could have said would have been a balm to my soul, soothing the bigotry and hate I'd experienced my whole fucking life with a single sentence.

Just one taste of her—that's all it took.

Just that one and I was lost.

KYLE—AFTER

I'm still staring into those amber depths until she face-plants into my chest and mumbles a sleepy "Morning."

Fuck, she's cute. I forgot how cute she was. Of all the things I remembered, this was the one I forgot. I forgot her rumpled mess of hair and the slight scrunch to her nose when she talked with morning breath. As if I gave a single fuck about that. I fought the urge to cup her face and kiss her like I did so many months ago. It seems like years since the first time my lips touched hers and even longer since the last time.

With Nicola's face in my chest, I look over her snarls of curls to see Willa slip into the room. Willa has checked Nicola over about twenty times since she woke for the first time yesterday, and other than the memory loss and some slight muscle atrophy, she has a clean bill of health. Nicola's walk is a little iffy, but the fact that she *can* walk is a major win. She's not at a Phoenix level of health, but she's alive and that is pretty much all I care about. The memories we can deal with.

"I'm going to the restroom," she mumbles into my chest and shakily removes herself from the bed to walk to the bathroom. When the door snicks closed, I notice Willa's face is full-scale freaked the fuck out.

"What?" I bark, my body going rigid and I'm on my feet in an instant.

"We have a huge fucking problem, Kyle," Willa blurts.

Before I can get the story, I hear Nicola screaming blue bloody murder in the bathroom. I try the door, but the handle doesn't turn. I don't think, putting my boot in the door and busting the lock to find Nic at the mirror gripping the sink for all she's worth. She's not looking at me or Willa—who is crowded in the bathroom behind me.

Nicola is staring at the mirror—staring but not actually seeing. I know for a fact now that the visions won't be an issue because I am one hundred percent certain I'm watching her have one right now.

As rivulets of blood fall from her tear ducts, all of me wishes this was the one thing that never came back.

5

NICOLA—AFTER

My boots pounded against the pavement as I ran through a deserted parking lot in the dead of night. The lot might be bereft of cars, but I wasn't alone. Kyle was running just behind me, unable to travel due to the wide open wound in his gut. Kyle should have been able to pass me, he should be able to leave this place altogether—and would have if he hadn't put himself in between me and the monsters chasing us. Kyle took the clawed swipe meant for me and damn near died doing it.

We couldn't stop. I reach back to grab his hand and yank him along as I sprint toward the safe ground of the hospital. We did what we thought was best, but we shouldn't have left the grounds. We should have come up with a better plan.

I easily pick up the snarling breaths of wolves at our back. They were so close, so close. Then, Kyle stumbles just behind me, nearly pulling me down with him. My grip breaks on his hand, and I feel lost without it.

"Go, Nic! Run!" he roars, and I don't know what to do.

They don't want him. They wouldn't have hurt him if it weren't for me. I turn back to see Kyle on his hands and knees on the pavement, a single arm hugging his middle. His eyes plead with me, begging me to listen, and just this once, I do. I turn on my booted foot and sprint for the light.

When his agonized scream slams into me, I stumble, hitting the asphalt quicker than I can blink. The world spins slowly off its axis, and his scream is replaced with a sharp ringing in my ears. They caught us, they caught us.

Oh nonononononono...

I look back, praying to everything holy that I'm wrong. But I'm not.

Two of the wolves are still coming for me, yes, but the third? The third has his maw in Kyle's belly, shaking and shredding the muscle and tender tissue. And he's screaming. He's screaming...

My body feels like it is being ripped in half, my heart and my brain are all trying to deny what I'm seeing.

The two wolves coming for me leap, their form fading into a black mist before touching back down on the pavement into their human forms. There is no smile or joy to their faces, just cold, hard wrath.

The beat of my heart—once galloping from exertion—slows farther and farther until it is barely beating at all in my chest. My breaths slow, and I am almost grateful that I'm dying. I feel in my heart, Kyle is gone. I feel lucky to follow him.

Before I take what I know is my last breath, I do it staring into unearthly yellow eyes.

COLD WATER MEETS MY FACE AS I SNAP OUT OF WHAT CAN only be assumed as a vision. Curled on my side into a ball on the floor of the shower, I let the frigid water chase away the images still branded in my mind. My vision blurred, I blink several times before the room comes into focus.

Kyle, who in no way could ever possibly fit in the narrow stall with me, is kneeling on tile lip of the shower, his knees soaked from the spray. His hulking body is strung tight, nearly vibrating, but the tired dip to his eyes behind the thick frames of his glasses tell me he's seen this before. Fates know what I look like, curled up like a damn cat in this puny excuse for a shower. I probably seem like a crazy drowned rat. So far he's seen me hyperventilate myself into passing out, have a panic attack of epic proportions, unconsciously hurt myself, scream like a crazy woman, and now... passing out from the vision from hell. If I were him, I'd run screaming in the other direction.

What man in his right mind would sign up for this kind of mess?

"Are visions always like this?" I croak, shivering in the now biting water. It takes him a few minutes to respond. I can't tell if he's deciding on what to say to me or if he's just trying to find the right temperature for the water as he fiddles with the dial, but his response tells me I've put him through hell.

"No, babe. Not all of them are that bad," Kyle murmurs, his eyes never quite meeting mine. I swear there is a little ding in my brain telling me he's lying— telling me he's seen so much worse. In the very depths of my soul, I hoped I was wrong.

"Liar," I scold gently, earning me a wry smile and a nod as he finally quits with the tap and looks at me. I put a shaky hand to the shower floor and lever myself up to sitting.

"What did you see?" Kyle asks, his voice a rumbling whisper. I don't want to answer him. If I answer him, it might make it come true, and I don't want to watch him die again. I don't want those men or whoever they were to find us.

Not ever.

I don't want him to die because of me. Because the one thing I am absolutely certain of in all of this is that I'm the reason. Whatever happened, whatever brought me here to this hospital is my fault. I know in my gut those wolves were after me and not him. I won't put him in danger—even if it is to save me.

"I-I don't know. Most of it was too dark to see. It doesn't make much sense to me," I offered, hoping my voice doesn't betray me and I'm lucky because he gives me an out.

"That's okay, Shortcake. I wasn't sure you'd get the visions back at all. Maybe your body needs time to adjust."

I really fucking hope not. If these visions got any more detailed, I'd be carted off to the loony bin faster than I could freaking blink. I've more than likely booked my one-way ticket there already.

It was then I noticed how close to naked I was in my now see-through hospital gown—the water soaking the thin material and turning it into a freaking peep-show attraction. Fantastic. My arms fly to cover my exposed chest, and even though I know I'm technically married to this man, I'm not even in the vicinity of comfortable right now.

I don't know him; I don't know anyone, I tell myself.

But his eyes... his eyes say they've seen all of me before and love what they see. They say he's been starved for months and it's Sunday fucking dinner. Those eyes hit a nerve in me, and I don't know if I want him to act on all the promises those eyes are making or if I should still be mortified I'm practically naked in front of him.

"Move it or lose it, big man," Willa orders him, coming to my rescue. She shoves and prods him until he has no choice but to climb to his considerable height and exit the bathroom. Before he does, I get another heated look that is only tempered slightly by concern as he shuts the door with its now busted lock.

Willa says nothing as she helps me to my feet, makes sure I'm steady and passes toiletries through the half-closed curtain to me as I shower. She does, however, give me her dreaded eyebrow. I loathe that expression already, and I've known her for approximately twenty-four hours.

When I think Kyle's finally out of earshot, I whisper, "What?"

Her head tilts just to the side as her eyes flash green for a moment. She seems to consider me for a moment.

"You lied to him," she accuses

"Of course I lied to him!" I furiously whisper before the memory hits me like a slap in the face and it becomes impossible to stop the tears.

"I... I saw him die. I saw us both die. And it's my fault. They weren't coming for him."

"Who wasn't coming for him?" she asks, her body alert and tense.

"W-wolves," I say, my voice barely audible and watch as her eyes begin to glow.

"I need you to tell me exactly what happened in your vision, Nicola."

"We were off the hospital grounds, and they came and they... and they..." I can't finish that sentence before the horror of it hits me.

My chest feels like it's caving in from the weight of the loss of him. But I shouldn't still feel this way, right? He isn't dead. Just because I saw it, doesn't mean it has to happen. Just because I felt his death in every single cell in my body, doesn't mean I can't stop it.

Right?

"I can't let him die, Willa," I murmur, choking back my emotions. I turn off the water, grab the towel to dry my skin. She puts a comforting hand on my shoulder.

"I know. I'm going to get you some dry clothes to wear, and we'll figure this out. Don't lose it just yet, okay?" Willa assures me as she gives me a quick hug and leaves the room.

She doesn't know. She didn't see. There is no way I'm letting what I saw to happen to him. I don't care what it takes.

I'm saving him, and I don't give a shit if I have to die to do it.

6

KYLE—AFTER

PACING THE SHORT LENGTH OF THE HOSPITAL ROOM IS ABOUT all I can do right now. My emotions are all over the place, ranging from the kind of lust that is close to driving me insane and scared as hell because I know she's lying to me.

If I didn't know Nicola, if I didn't know every single inch of her, I would have believed she couldn't remember her vision. But I do. I know every single tell, and my Shortcake is lying her ass off. She might not want to tell me, and that's okay. She's had to withhold her visions from me before, and I understand why. But she's never lied about it. That kind of shit not only pisses me off, it freaks me the fuck out.

Why did she lie to me?

The thought runs on a constant loop in my brain until Willa steps from the bathroom.

"I need to get her some clothes and then the three of us are going to sit down and have a talk," she says, her face a worried mess, her tall, lithe frame on edge.

"I have clothes here for her—what the fuck did you think I was doing when I left? What the hell is happening, Willa? I know she's lying to me," I say, crossing my arms.

"Yeah, she is, and for good fucking reason, too. I don't know everything, but if she doesn't feel safe, she isn't going to tell us shit. This vision is bad, Ky..." she trails off. Her shoulders twitch in her natural feline way.

"People are going to be coming for us, no fucking shit, Willa. I know there are going to be repercussions for Iva's trail of bodies. Now tell me the goddamn problem," I order, not giving a shit if I'm being an asshole. I pull my glasses from their perch on my nose and pinch the bridge between my eyes.

"It has to do with what I was coming here to tell you anyway. There are wolves at the boundary of the grounds. They can't come in because they intend harm, but... the others here are telling me she can't stay. Right now, you both are being asked to leave. The hospital and the grounds are only sanctuary for the ill. Iva won no favors from the coven keeping the ward."

Of course she didn't. Iva. Just that name makes my skin crawl.

"Fucking Witches and their goddamn rules," I mutter realizing the irony of my statement as I say it. *Fucking Witches when I'm part Witch.* If only it were a part of myself I could just cut off like a wart or a cancer, but no, it's me—even if it's the part of me I hate.

"Be that as it may, they will make you leave if they have to. Is there any place for you to go?"

"Yeah," I say, my fingers knifing through my hair and yanking the short strands.

I do have a place where we could go. I don't know if I want to go back there, though. I don't know if I ever want to see that house—my house—again.

It was my safe place.

It was where I kissed her the first time, where I made love to her for the first time. It was the only sanctuary I had.

It was ours—and they took it away from us.

KYLE—BEFORE

I'd never tasted something so good as Nicola's mouth.

Jesus, shit, fuck.

Never in my life had I had this driving need to kiss and consume and take. I wanted her more than I'd wanted anything ever in my whole fucking life. Sure, I'd bedded plenty of women, but this one tiny Phoenix kicked the shit out of every single memory in my head.

When her lips parted and her tongue met mine, the taste of her just got better. Woman and cinnamon.

Jesus, shit, fuck.

My hands threaded through her mass of hair, gently pulling her head back so I could get better access to that mouth. Her answering moan hit me right in the dick, and finally deciding the distance between our bodies was too great, I abandoned her hair for her waist. I ran my hands over her thin sundress, the heat of her body filtering through the fabric.

Hoisting her up so her chest rested against mine, I couldn't help the grin that pulled at my mouth when her arms wrapped around my neck and her legs circled my hips. Soon, her hands started to roam, pulling at clothes, unbuttoning, unzipping, exposing her pale, porcelain skin to my assuredly black gaze. Her dress hung on her waist, all that stopped me from seeing the rest of her upper body was the pale blue lace of a teeny strapless bra. I wanted the rest. I wanted all of her. I wanted her heat against my chest, my mouth, my hands.

I wanted to taste and touch all of her and so I did. I set her right there on the counter of my kitchen island, and my now free hands spanned the soft skin of her waist, my thumbs skating the underside of each breast. Her shudder and moan in response damn near killed me. Her legs widened and I fell between them, cursing the counter for not being a bed. My fingers curled over the top edge of the lace and I tugged at the fabric to expose the most perfect, delicately pink nipple attached to the best fucking breast I'd ever seen in my whole life.

My lips quickly found the peak and the moan that ripped up her throat damn near turned me feral. I fought the urge to bite, to mark that perfect skin to show anyone and everyone she was mine, and no one else could have her.

"Don't," she murmured, her voice a shaky whisper as her hands pulled my face from her breast. I stopped, my body strung tight and ready to break, but I stopped. I needed to cool myself down, but everything that was her called to me.

"Okay, baby. I'll stop," I said as I ran my nose up the column of her neck and rested my forehead against hers. I got a frustrated moan in response that only ignited me further.

"Not, *stop*, stop. Just don't bite," she explained as her hands drifted down my abs to my belt buckle.

Don't bite?

"I don't know how possible that is, Shortcake. In case you hadn't noticed, my response to you is not exactly rational."

She grabbed my face then, and in a rare moment of accuracy, her eyes met mine. At that moment, I felt all her attention on me—every single fiber of her being was centered on this, on us. I took in every fleck of blue in her eyes, and marveled at the red hue to her long eyelashes. I was laser focused on her, so I didn't miss it when her irises lit with a pale blue phosphorescent glow.

"Do your best, then. It's important, Kyle. Don't rush this," she demanded, her soft husky voice binding around my heart.

I thought I was lost before. I thought I'd already fallen down the rabbit hole. I had no idea how far I'd actually plummeted until that very second.

"I promise, Nic. I won't bite you unless I absolutely cannot stop myself. Just know, one day I will, and you'll be mine." She only smiled in response.

I should have known then.

TWO WEEKS. ALL WE GOT WAS TWO MEASLY WEEKS WHEN WE should have gotten forever. Hiding out in my cabin, we kissed, touched, fucked, made love, and talked for hours —only stopping to eat or for me to make a quick run for supplies. The last time—before everything went to hell —I came back to Nicola sitting on at the kitchen table playing the violin I'd procured for her a few days prior.

In getting to know her, I realized how much she missed her instruments—her piano and violin in particular. I couldn't carry a piano through the dense forest, but I could bring her a violin. I'd found one in a music store in Lexington, not realizing she would have preferred a used one to a brand spanking new violin. Nicola hadn't yet played for me, saying it took time to get to know the instrument before she played it. What she really meant was she wanted to break it in before I heard her.

Walking through the front door, I immediately recognized the song she was playing, 'Farewell' by Apocalyptica. Although the song was made for the deep strains of a cello, she did it justice with her expert skill. Each sweep of her bow and finger vibrato just about broke my heart. Somehow, she poured even more emotion into the song, and I was overcome with an intense feeling of loss. It was like she was telling me goodbye.

As beautiful as the song was, I fucking hated it.

Two goddamn weeks had passed and she still hadn't let me bind her. I was frustrated, but with each passing day I feared there was a reason she wouldn't let me. I feared she'd be ripped away from me.

I should have known.

I FELT HER STIR IN THE DEAD OF NIGHT. SHE SHOULD HAVE been exhausted—I knew I was—from our acrobatics a few hours prior, but she slipped from the bed and felt her way to the kitchen.

I followed her silently, as only a Wraith can, to the kitchen table and watched as she sat naked on the dining chair. Her pale skin glowed from the scant moonlight filtering through the window, her hair a rumpled mass of snarls and curls. She seemed to be readying herself for something, and as fascinating as her naked body was, my unease grew with each passing second.

Something was wrong.

Suddenly, she slapped a hand over her mouth and gripped the table for all she was worth. Her body arching with the strain, her eyes flashed open, glowing bright blue. I'd seen Aurelia's eyes glow like that when she was in the middle of a vision—but never Nicola's. She hadn't had a single one since she'd been here, and the force of them scared the shit out of me.

Then she started screaming, the sound barely muffled by her hand as her body convulsed from whatever she was seeing. I couldn't let her go through it alone. Hell, it was why I got up with her in the first place, but I couldn't just stand there watching.

Crossing the room, I grabbed the hand which had been latched to the table and immediately regretted my decision. The force of her grip was tighter than a vice and I felt my bones creak from the pressure.

"Nicola, baby, I need you snap out of it!" I ordered shaking her hand, but Nicola remained in her vision, tears of blood falling from her eyes.

I did the only thing I could.

I scooped her into my arms and held her until it was over. It seemed like hours that her body was a tense wire of agony, but in reality, it was probably only a few more minutes. Finally, her body relaxed and her eyes closed, squeezing out several more blood tears.

"K-Ky?" Nicola croaked when she came back to herself.

"You scared the shit out of me, Shortcake," I murmured in her hair, as I kissed her temple.

"Ky?" she repeated, her body shivering even though the heat of her felt like she would burst into her Fireskin at any given second.

"Yeah, baby," I answered. I didn't know if she couldn't hear me or if my voice just wasn't registering in her brain, but really, she was just trying to get me to pay attention.

"Men are coming... Here... Th-they are coming. Do-don't have m-much time. Ge-get dressed. Run. Th-they will use you against me," she haltingly explained but her words didn't make sense to me.

"Nic, no one can get through the wards without me knowing, and no one knows where we are, baby."

"They have Witches with them. They found you. They can break the ward. They are going to kill you, Ky. Ge-get b-bloody dressed and get out of here!" she shouted.

Then I felt the ward break—a shiver of a burning ripple flashed across my skin.

They were already here.

7

NICOLA—AFTER

SHIVERING IN A TOWEL. NO, SHIVERING IN A *GODDAMN* TOWEL, sitting on a toilet seat in a hospital bathroom when I should be getting as far from Kyle as humanly possible.

Oh, that's right. You're not human, a snide voice in my head reminded me. Not that I had any frame of reference on what being human meant, but I bet my lily-pale ass it didn't mean watching my quasi-husband being gutted by a fucking werewolf. Or having visions about said gutting that made my eyes literally bleed.

I needed clothes. I needed a plan. I needed to not be a brainless fucking idiot and get a damn clue.

Preferably in that order.

A soft knock on the door proceeds Kyle poking his

head in, a stack of clothes in his arms. Fabulous, one problem down, five million to go.

"I had clothes here for you just in case you woke up," he says as he offers the small pile of cloth in his hands to me. "You can get other clothes if you don't like these—just say the word."

I try to study the bundle in his arms but can't seem to tear my eyes away from his hands. I don't know what it is about them that catches my interest. Is it the rough but long-fingered grace to them? Is it the way they seem to have seen the sun and wind and earth of this world and yet seem so gentle?

I know what it is. It's the way his hand pressed to his belly in my vision. It's the way the blood oozed in between the gaps in his fingers, staining the webbings red. It's the way they laid lifeless on the pavement as that fucking wolf ripped into him, only moving with the force from the jerks of its teeth tearing his body apart.

It takes effort to tear my eyes from them and grab the bundle from his hands, mumbling a quick thank you as I turn away. I have to take deep breaths to quell the nausea in my stomach and the bile coming up my throat.

I am the reason. It will be my fault. I have to go, I have to go, I have to go...

Before he leaves me to it, he asks, "You okay, Shortcake?"

Am I okay? Did he not see me cry fucking blood not ten minutes ago?

"I'm bloody fucking super, alright?" I snap and immediately feel bad for it. He doesn't know what I saw, and if I have any say at all, he won't know ever.

"I'm sorry," I whisper, "I'm... not dealing very well, okay?"

I wait for him to yell at me and I assume he might or leave me to my bitchy temper tantrum, but he doesn't. Kyle heaves a sigh before his heat meets my back and his lips brush the top of my hair. "I can understand that. Get dressed, babe, and we'll work it out, okay?"

I nod, and after hearing the broken door close, I drop my towel and inspect my body for the first time. My skin is porcelain pale without a single freckle. The only thing marring it that I can see is a double crescent scar on the meat of my hand. If I didn't know better, I would say the scar looked like someone or something took a chunk out of me. My mind drifts back to the wolves, and I shudder.

I examine the clothing Kyle gave me. The soft gray, knit fabric appears to be a shirt. The pants are made of a thick, dark denim. In between the shirt and the pants is a small bundle of dark gray lace and my brain finally supplies the word—undergarments. I thrust my legs into the lace panties, slip into the bra and then try to figure out the shirt. The thin knit feels smooth against my skin, and once I find the tag and figure out how I should put it on, I realize the draping of the fabric is what held me up. The shirt is a slit-neck sweater, the right shoulder ruched and draping diagonally across my body into an asymmetrical hemline. I take a look at it in the mirror and am surprised at the elegance of it. It looked much more complicated than it was. The pants were easier to figure out—I slipped into the skinny jeans with much less confusion.

Sufficiently dressed, I hunted up a hairbrush and began the attack on my curls before giving up and braiding a few sections of hair away from my face. Shrugging since this was the best it was going to get, I emerge from the bathroom barefoot to the ripe tenseness of my hospital room.

Kyle and Willa are facing off like a pair of pissed off lions. In Willa's case, I am almost certain she is a shifter cat of some sort. The deep guttural growl in her throat was in no way human.

I wonder if I can slip out of this room without either of them noticing?

I was able to eye the door for about three seconds before Kyle's voice snaps me back to the room.

"Don't even think about it," his rumbling growl whips at me, paired with the bulging biceps from his crossed arms and a look that is part exasperation and part utter fury.

Shit! How did he know?

"What? I shouldn't look for an exit before the two of you rip each other apart? Please excuse me for have a modicum of self-preservation instincts," I reply, crossing my arms to match his, squaring my shoulders and hips to show him I am in no way cowed.

"No, you should stop acting shifty as fuck," he growls at me, his eyes flashing from chocolate to inky black and back again. I should be scared—I really should—but I'm not. Now, I'm just pissed off.

"Because I looked for the bloody door?" I ask, bewildered.

"No, because you lied to me, searched for the fucking exit *and* won't answer my goddamn questions," he replies, his voice rising and his hold on calm slipping.

"Maybe it's because I don't. Fucking. Know. You. I don't know her," I say gesturing to Willa. "I don't know my own bloody last name. Maybe because I have no idea if I can trust you. Or what put me in this hospital. Or what I like or don't like. When I was born or who I fucking am," I reply honestly. I don't know if I can trust him—I just know I have to save his life.

Trust is not in the equation at all.

"You said you didn't want to know!" he yells in exasperation, his grip on calm lost to his temper.

"Well, I reserve the right to change my bloody mind!" I volley back realizing too late that we have squared off and are nose to nose, him leaning down to my level.

"I swear to the fucking Fates if I didn't love you so goddamn much I would wring your damn neck. What did you see, Nicola? We don't have time for you to weigh the pros and cons of telling me. Forewarning is *always* better. Stop hoarding everything you see. Maybe you can change this one for fuck's sake."

His words hit me right in the gut, and all of a sudden I want to cry. I can't process the love comment. How could he possibly? I can't be the woman he fell in love with.

I don't even know who that woman was.

I meet his eyes, mine burning with unshed tears—tears I refuse to lose my hold on. "I saw you die. You were mauled by what I can only guess is a werewolf. You tried to save me and got yourself killed. Is that what you want to know?" I ask, defeated.

I just wanted him safe. Is that so bad?

Kyle's face shuts down, the black of his eyes—which had bled all the way through his sclera—flick back to chocolate. His nod comes next and then Kyle turns from me and walks right out the door, leaving me and Willa in his wake.

"He's a hothead. Leave him be and he'll calm down on his own," Willa's voice breaks the silence.

"Sure," I murmur, still staring at the door.

"I'm going to ready your discharge papers. Sit tight, okay?"

I nod as she leaves the room, but I have absolutely no intention of staying put. First order of business, find shoes. Second, get the fuck out of here. I start searching the room for anything and everything, starting with the drawers resting just under the dark window ledge.

The first drawer is socks, underwear, bras and sleepwear. Piles of them in my size. Interesting. The second is shirts, pants, skirts—all carefully folded. The third and final drawer is filled with shoes, a slouchy purse and an empty duffle bag.

I yank out the duffle, filling it with the clothes and shoes, dropping a single pair of black leather flats on the floor and slipping into them as I work. Then, I inspect the purse. It is a buttery black leather with large circles connecting the single strap to the bulk of the bag. In it is a matching thin zippered wallet, a tiny paisley printed bag filled with hair stuff, a small bag of makeup—the tubes all still sealed—and a mechanical device of some sort. My brain supplies the word—phone. Weird. There are no number buttons and except for a single button in the bottom middle and a few on the sides, there is nothing else. I have no freaking idea how to work it.

I drop the phone back in the purse, zip it and heft the duffle on my shoulder, finding it much lighter than I thought it would be. I remember the crap in the bathroom and dash to grab it, shoving the tubes of stuff in the bag and getting the hell out of there.

I crack the door and peer out to a well-lit hallway. At the far end of the hall, Willa stands at a counter talking to another woman. I breathe a sigh of relief when Kyle is nowhere to be found. I see a bright red exit sign hanging from the ceiling to my right, so I open the door wider and slip through, letting it quietly snick shut before calmly walking toward the sign.

I follow the arrow to another door labeled 'stairs' and silently press the lever. As soon as the door is open wide enough I slip through and catch it before it slams. I think I'm home free—Willa didn't see me and Kyle is gone to Fates knew where—when suddenly, a hand latches onto my right bicep and yanks me around to face a smiling woman.

She is tall, blue-haired and tattooed on almost every inch of available skin except for her face, neck and hands. Her makeup is freaking flawless with a pretty red pout and eyeliner I couldn't duplicate if my life depended on it.

She's dressed in light-wash cuffed skinny jeans, a black tank top that reads 'Live Fast, Die Pretty' in a circle of words with a skull and crossed lipsticks instead of crossbones in the center. All of this is under a cropped, three-quarter sleeve black leather jacket that I'm sure I'd sell my first-born for.

She makes me look dull and frumpy. And short. Especially when I get a glimpse at her fire engine red, double strap, sky-high Mary Jane pumps.

I can't remember my last name but I know what those shoes are called. That's some priorities right there.

She has to be the most colorfully cool person I have ever seen—not that I've seen many people. She thrusts out her hand to shake and introduces herself.

"Hi, my name is Max. Your cousin called in a favor. I'm here to save your ass."

I have a cousin? That strikes me as information I probably should have been told. Like, *'hey here's your husband and by the way, you have family waiting in the wings you also don't remember.'*

"Cousin? I have family?" I ask because, well, no one else mentioned this.

"Yeah. You do. Aurelia's on her honeymoon with her hunky hubby and their kiddos, otherwise she'd be here herself. She called yesterday and I hauled my ass here from Denver to come get you. She said you had a wolf problem. Do you... Are you okay?" she asks—either because I am *this-close* to either hyperventilating or losing my mind.

Maybe both.

"I really wish people would stop asking me that when they bloody well know the answer. No. No, I am not okay. I have zero memory, I had to figure out how to put on clothes, and my 'husband' is a big jerk whose life I have to save. I am a huge ball of not fucking okay."

"Well, honey, let's get out of here and then you can tell Momma Max all about it," she says as she takes the duffle off my shoulder and puts it on her own, throws an arm around my shoulders and guides me down the stairs.

8

KYLE—AFTER

She is doing this for me—lying for me, protecting me. Again. The last time she protected me, she ripped everything I loved away in a single vicious jerk. I don't know what she thinks she's protecting me from this time, well, I do, but I don't understand it.

Wolves. Of the number of factions Iva wronged, the wolves wouldn't have been my guess of the first ones to come after her. I would have thought it would have been the Witches.

Witches were the ones who stormed our house. They were the ones who broke my ward—the ones who brought us to the Wraiths who beat and tortured us.

They were the ones who betrayed one of their own kind. They were the ones who betrayed me and mine.

KYLE—BEFORE

We dressed as fast as we could, arming ourselves with the limited arsenal I had on hand. Breaking three floorboards to get to the cache I'd hidden in my bedroom—a single Glock and three mags.

It wasn't enough.

I never thought anyone would be able to break the ward. I thought we were safe. I thought I could protect her. For only being half-Witch, I am more potent a caster than most. My Wraith side lends power to my spells—the more fed I was, the stronger I would be— and the day before I cast the warding spell, I'd just glutted myself on the fallen souls of a nasty prison riot. I didn't take them all, of course, just the most rancid.

We Wraiths take the term sin-eater seriously.

But I'd put too much confidence in myself and didn't plan ahead—I was a fucking idiot.

Nicola told me Witches were with the men coming for us, told me about Evangeline and Iva, and so many things that didn't seem to register in my fool brain. It didn't even cross my mind that they would hurt one of their own or break the cardinal rule of a Witch's ward.

I'm a half-breed, sure, but my grandmama told me I would be accepted—that Witches never hurt their own. Ridicule, demean, and ostracize them maybe, but never physically hurt them.

I suppose their agenda didn't include me or my heritage because they plowed through my ward like it was nothing—like the boundary of my land was as inconsequential as a line in the sand. Wards are sacred —they are never meant to be crossed. These Witches held no honor.

One second the ward broke, and the next, Nicola was screaming at me to run—grabbing my shoulders, her eyes aglow with a new vision, fresh tears of blood falling down her face.

"No, Shortcake. It is my job to protect you," I argued. There was no way I was leaving her there to deal with the lot of them by herself. They would hurt her—hurt my woman, my mate. Bound or not, she was mine and I wouldn't leave her. Never—but especially not to save my own hide. What kind of coward would that make me?

"There is no protecting me, Ky," she whispered, "Get out of here. Please!" Her voice was like molasses over gravel with the way it broke.

What the fuck did she mean there was no protecting her?

"Wha-" I began, but I couldn't finish the question

before every single window and door blew in—the shards of wood and glass peppering us like shrapnel. I threw my body over Nic's, absorbing the concussion of the spell, not realizing she didn't need to be protected at all.

Nicola slipped from beneath my heavy, stunned body, ripped the Glock from the back of my pants and started shooting. Blind as she was, I never thought she could defend herself. Hell, that was why I spirited her away here—because I thought Nicola couldn't fight at all. She said herself she was no good in a fight. I didn't understand how she could shoot with any accuracy, but her aim was true.

Eyes aglow, Nicola's paisley print dress swished around her thighs as she moved around me barefoot to take a few more shots—the bullets finding their homes in the skulls of three men who were unfortunate enough to set one single foot into this house. But she couldn't catch them all, and soon she was down, a bullet in her right shoulder.

Before I could catch my bearings—before I could get to her—two sets of hands hauled me up, and the cold steel of a curved blade pressed into my throat hard enough to draw blood. A woman stood before me holding the blade—severe face, ash-blonde hair, black on black suit, and so painfully gaunt it was a wonder how she was still standing. Her face was impassive, caring not for the situation or the fact that she was holding the blade cutting into me.

I was nothing to her, a tool to be used.

"Stop! Do-don't hurt him!" Nicola screamed, and the woman's face finally cracked a smile, proving the tool theory.

"But of course, darling, I have no intention of hurting him, but you need to do me a favor first," the woman said with a sick twist to her lips.

"What do you want?" Nicola growled through clenched teeth shrugging off the hands that held her to dig her fingers into the gunshot wound in her arm— pulling the bullet out with her fingertips and dropping it on the floor. The wound began to close almost immediately, and Nicola settled in to wait—the woman's eyes riveted on the knitting flesh.

"I need you to do what we say, when we say. Do you think you can do that?" When she received no reply, she added, "We'll be taking your lover with us as insurance, of course."

At those words, I tried to get the hands off of me, but a few whispered words from the blonde woman and my body went lax without my consent. My body may have been slack, but my mind was sharp and focused on Nicola. I wanted to tell her no. I wanted to tell her there was no way this ended happily and to get the hell away from these people—but my mouth refused to work, sealed shut by the same spell that kept me lethargic.

Nicola was silent—either contemplating the woman's request or waiting for her wound to finish closing so she could kill them all—I didn't know which. She stood proudly, head held high, her body straight if a little bloody from the fight, her hair a wild snarl around her shoulders and face. Nicola's blue eyes lit up again, and she met the woman's eyes with surprising accuracy.

"Tessa, is it? I want you to remember something for me. You can kill and maim and torture, but when the end comes, everything burns. Including you. When *your* end comes, remember I told you that."

KYLE—AFTER

Nicola foretold Tessa's death—I could remember that now that Tessa was dead—by fire just as Nicola said she would.

I couldn't remember Tessa's face until after she died —a spell no doubt to make me forget. Clever Witch to make such a spell for a man she had no intention of ever seeing the light of day again. It was a cover your ass spell if I ever saw one. It made sure that I didn't rip her apart as soon as I saw her ugly fucking face.

I clench my fists, and hiss as the bite of my talons gouge my palms. I have to get it together. I am not a help to anyone if I lose my temper. I look out into the night sky from my perch on a lonely wooden bench in the courtyard at the center of the hospital. If I didn't know Witches warded the place, I could have guessed by the herbs, flowers, and trees planted here. The hospital walls reached for the sky, but if I hadn't walked through the sterile corridor to get here, I would never know I was on a hospital's grounds.

The four exterior walls were covered in thick vines. On the north one grew Clematis, the pink summer flowers still blooming at the end of October. Bright purple Wisteria covered the west one, blue Morning Glories the south and tiny white Jasmine flowers populated the east. Raised beds full of blooming flowers lined the walls, trees dotting the corners, and all the while—even in the midst of what should be my people's work—I couldn't help but feel alone.

Nicola sacrificed for me—did things she hated because they needed to be done. Even when she had no memory of us and what we meant to each other, she still tried to protect me. It pisses me off that she is the only one who has to make these sacrifices.

But she is.

Nicola's making these moves because she thinks she has to... *And I just left her there. I'm a fucking idiot.*

I have to get over my own shit. She needs me and I left her there like an asshole.

I check my surroundings to make sure the coast is clear before traveling directly to Nicola's room. It's probably stupid of me. She has absolutely no frame of reference to grasp what she would be seeing when a swath of black smoke fills her room, but honestly, I don't have time to trek through the entire hospital. It's already bad enough that I have to say sorry, to ask me to stand in an elevator with strangers is pushing it.

I expect a gasp from her—or a scream—but I get nothing. I get nothing because the room is empty. I check the bathroom—nothing. And then my eyes snag on the open and suspiciously empty dresser drawers.

Motherfucker. I should have known she would bolt.

Well, it wasn't the first time I needed to find my woman and given the fiery temper that matched her deep red hair, it wouldn't be the last.

At least I'm good at finding things.

9

NICOLA—AFTER

MAX AND I WALK DOWN THE STAIRS—ALL NINE FLIGHTS OF them—to get to the main entrance. With every step I take, I feel colder and colder—my chest twisting the closer we get to the front door. I don't know what was waiting out there for us.

"Did my cousin tell you what the wolf problem was?" I ask Max.

"She sure did. She said Kyle was going to eat it and because he had been very naughty you were going to eat it too, so I had better haul ass to Knoxville so you didn't die."

I didn't even remotely understand that convoluted sentence. *Kyle was naughty? Eat it? What the hell?*

"Is that all she told you?"

"No," she replies simply.

"Care to elaborate?" I press.

"She said I was supposed to punch Kyle in the junk the next time I saw him for her."

Well, alright then.

"Anything else?"

"Nope. That about covers it," she says as we march through the automatic doors toward the parking lot, not stopping or slowing down until we reach a gleaming, cherry red car.

Max snaps her fingers and with a tiny flash of green, the door locks disengage. I feel my eyebrows reach my hairline as I gape at her.

"What? It's more effective than an alarm," she says as she shrugs, opening the driver side door and tossing my bag in the backseat of the low-slung, tough-as-nails car.

"What is this?" I ask pointing at the beauty reverently.

"A 1971 Chevy Chevelle SS," she says with a little grin that tells me she's about to scare the shit out of me driving this car.

I'm not wrong.

"Hold onto your tits, baby girl. I'm about to knock your socks off," Max informs me as we slide in and she turns the key, igniting the demon who lives in the engine. Holy balls.

"Buckle up, buttercup. We need to haul ass," Max says as she glances at the rearview mirror.

I do as instructed and Max peels out of the spot as if her ass is on fire, fishtailing through the narrow-lane parking lot until she reaches the main thoroughfare. Then, Max really opens her up, the demon in the engine growling a guttural song of speed and agility.

Max at the wheel is frightening, but in such a way that I enjoy the thrill—even if I might die at any moment. We pass cars and trucks, merging onto a freeway and cutting off four cars in the process.

"I need to tell you something," Max says, the reluctance in her voice scaring the shit out of me.

"What?"

"We may or may not have a car following us."

"We *may* have a car following us?" I parrot back.

"Okay, okay. We do have a car following us, and I will bet you all the money I own—which is a considerable amount—that it isn't your husband."

Several things occur to me all at once: A—it still irks me to call Kyle my husband, B—I don't have any money, not that I would ever bet against her, C—given that I have no funds, no memory and limited avenues to ask for help, my escape attempt may have been ill-advised, and D—we have people following us and that is a very bad thing.

"And why would you say that?" I ask, my voice surprisingly calm considering the circumstances. I swear, Max is the least forthcoming person I've ever met. Seeing as I know exactly three people, that isn't saying much, but could a woman spell it out?

"Because they've been following us since we left the hospital and you have a wolf problem. Ergo, wolves are more than likely following us."

"We've been driving for fifteen minutes, and you're just now saying something?" I screech.

"I didn't want to worry you," Max says as she shrugs, making a sharp turn to the wheel and cutting off two cars and an enormous truck to get to an exit on the freeway from the far left lane.

"Well, that's fucking comforting!" I yell, my hands scrambling to hold onto the door handle.

Max blows through a red light and makes a sharp left turn that has the back wheels of the car fighting for purchase on the road. Soon, we are traveling down a pitch-black, two-lane road—the lights of the city far behind us.

"Do you think we lost them?" I ask after a solid stretch of no lights behind us.

Max shrugs, flips her headlights off and guns the engine in the darkness, earning a screech from me.

"What are you doing?" I yell, my hands frantically searching for something to hold onto. It didn't matter that I already had a death-grip on the upholstery.

"I'm trying to keep us both breathing. I can see in the dark. Problem is, so can they. I think I lost them back at the freeway, but it won't hurt to go dark for a bit to make su-"

Max doesn't even get to finish her sentence before lights flash on in the oncoming lane—about two seconds before the enormous truck the lights are attached to slams into the front end of our car.

I don't even have time to scream.

NICOLA—OREGON 1855

You can tell a lot by the way a person fulfills a promise. I promised Rhys that Aurelia would live—I bound them on purpose so she would, so she could do the work I couldn't. I found early on, keeping this promise would be the death of me.

I've never had a Soldier—never needed one. In the beginning, Soldiers were a way to help the newly blind Oracles adjust to their circumstances. I had always been blind, and never needed someone to help me to figure out how to cut my food or fetch water or make my way around our village. I didn't need help. It was a rare occasion for me not to know what was in my path or what was coming next.

I wasn't made an Oracle—I was born one. As a child it was harder—I only saw deaths. I never knew what was coming, but as I grew, so did my abilities. I knew much more than my Oracle sisters. Sisters is what Iva called them—I had none by blood. I had no family except for a distant uncle who refused to see me. Kale Constantine was my mother's half-brother, and his two daughters, my cousins—Aurelia and Mena—would be our race's salvation.

I'd seen it.

The trouble was, keeping these two alive was an exercise in patience and would cost me. Dearly.

I stood in the blackness of an alcove—the lanterns I'd snuffed out myself—the only light coming from my illuminated eyes. Their glow was faint, so when the Soldier came—stumbling and floundering through the darkness, it was easy to cut him down. I refused to kill him, so I made sure the blade in my hand was pure silver instead of the Morganite that would rob him of his life completely.

I had to pave the way for Rhys. He would be injured and not at his full strength.

I grabbed ahold of the fallen Soldier, his name I could not recall, and threw him over my shoulder to dispose of him out of the pathway. I had much more work to do.

NICOLA—OREGON 1965

I was the damn Devil—the absolute worst sort of person—someone who did nothing while others were suffering. Biding my time was one thing, but... Iva was hurting her, starving her, draining her. Letting others hurt her.

And I did nothing. I didn't stop Iva, or the guard who stole Mena's innocence. I didn't feed her. I didn't release her. When I died, I would reside in the lowest pit of Hell.

"Mena," I whispered into the pitch that was Mena's cell. I'd been whispering her name over and over, since I slipped in this vile, stinking hovel an hour ago. She'd been catatonic for days now, not eating the meager scraps of food the guards brought, not sleeping, not blinking.

If she weren't breathing, I'd swear she was dead.

"Mena. I need you to listen to me. I need you to understand," I murmured urgently. My time was almost up. Soon, someone would be checking on me and I couldn't afford to be missing. I had to say what I came there to say. I had to give her hope where she had none.

"I have done horrible things. I have neglected you, and for that I am sorry. But I will do anything to save this Legion. I will manipulate, and sacrifice, and I will kill to save them. I will sacrifice a few to save many. I will do horrible things for the greater good," I told her, unsure if she heard me or if none of my words penetrated the haze of guilt and fear that clouded her mind.

"And you can hate me for that. I hate me for that. And after all I've done, I will probably go straight to hell once this life is finished," I admitted, "And I will accept it because in this life I was given, I did not choose my path, but I accept my destiny. So, you can dislike me, even hate me, all you want. I accept that. But I will save them. I will make sure that they are on the right path. I will bring them back from the darkness."

"But I need your help," I pleaded, "I need you to stay here. I need you to endure this hell, and I will help you when I can."

Fates, how could I ask this of her? How could I ask this of anyone? How could I possibly keep her alive?

"Your sister is coming. Not for a while, but she is," I assured her, "I need you to stay here until she gets you out. And when you get out, I need you to leave her and hide. People will come for you. They will try and steal you and make you a slave to feed their thirst for power. I need you to hide until Evangeline Marie Black has been made the Wraith Queen. When she's made Queen, go to her and help her. She will make sure Iva dies and stays dead. Do whatever you can to help her. And once Iva is gone, make sure you live. Live for all the time we stole from you and all the pain we caused."

Tears clogged my throat, but they were as worthless and I was right then. What could I offer her to assuage this pain? A promise? And what good would it be if I failed her.

I will not fail this girl, I promised myself. I won't.

"Stay strong, cousin," I murmured as I pressed a kiss to her forehead, the faint buzz of power tickled my lips.

She would live. I didn't care who I had to kill to make sure of it, but I'd fight an army to keep my fucking promise.

IO

NICOLA—AFTER

THE CAR CRUMPLES IN SLOW MOTION, THE CONCUSSION OF impact rippling through the cherry-red metal and us like a wave rolling into the shore. The windshield shatters, raining glass down on us, metal fuses to metal, and Max and I are thrown around the cab like pebbles in an empty tin can.

In the aftermath, confused and aching, my first thought is to reach for Max. She is unconscious, her lax body crumpled over the steering wheel, blood dripping from the wide open gash on her forehead. We are lucky we were wearing our seatbelts, and that the heavy construction of the car could stop a tank. I unbuckle my belt and scoot across the bench seat to check her pulse. I feel the steady beat going strong, but she's still in bad shape. I need to stop the bleeding.

My brain—muddled from the impact—finally catches on that we weren't the only ones in the accident. My eyes drift to the truck that hit us and it dawns on me that the only light is coming from the empty cab of their truck, the driver and passenger doors thrown wide.

Weapons. I need weapons. Danger! my mind screams.

I check under my seat only to find nothing. The glove compartment is empty as well. Deciding the only other place the weapons could be hiding is in the trunk, I go to open the door, only to find it harder than it should be. Looking down to inspect myself, I just now notice a twisted shard of metal sticking out of my right shoulder. As thick as marker and just about as long, the blackened piece of metal could have come from the engine or maybe from the crumpled front hood.

I guess it's lucky I'm left-handed. The thought floats through my brain. I don't know where it came from or how I know that, but I'll take it. Being left-handed will be a virtue right about now.

It takes me a while to realize it doesn't hurt. *That's bad. It should really hurt,* I think and deliberate with myself on the merits of pulling it out. The shard is impaled dead-center, and it's deep—going through bone and completely obliterating the joint. Looking down at it, I think I'm glad it doesn't hurt, because when it does, it is going to be awful.

Shock. You are going into shock.

Something catches my eye out of the passenger-side window—a slinking gray shadow flitting through the blackness. Shit. It is enough to snap me out of my stupor.

I look back to Max, praying for some magical back-up, but she's still passed out and bleeding, her face a macabre mask of blood. It's then that my eye snags on the blissfully filled dash holster. My left hand reaches for it, thumbing off the holster snap and pulling the Glock from its home. My fingers move without my brain telling them to, checking the mag and painfully chambering a round.

Feeling like a sitting duck, I turn in my seat plant both feet in the door, shoving it open. It takes too much out of me, and when I climb out, I find myself sagging against the side of the car. My knees are a pitiful show of strength.

Keep Max safe. She can't defend herself. Keep her safe, my brain supplies idiotically, and I try to quiet my mind and breathing to listen for the pad of wolf feet over the incessant dinging coming from the truck's open doors.

The growl that meets my ears sends a chill down my

spine but gives me the information I need. My left arm rises and my finger squeezes the trigger an instant too late. My bullet meets nothing but air as the wolf turns from his animal self into incorporeal smoke, landing with his hand around my throat before I can get off another shot.

He's tall, with scraggly blond hair reaching his chin, eyes the color of amber and a scar as thick as a pencil running from his hairline, through his eyebrow, skipping his eye, before continuing down his cheek and curving through his upper lip. His hot, putrid breath skates across my skin as he takes a long sniff up my neck.

"You smell different, but I know it's you," he whispers in my ear with a thick southern drawl as he tightens his hold on my throat, adding a crippling grip on my wrist forcing me to drop the gun.

"She smells much better now. I bet she'll taste real nice," a second man chimes in.

Damn, I was hoping there was only one.

The first thing I notice isn't his features or his clothes, no, the first thing I notice is the thick blade of the hunting knife he's using to clean the dirt from under his filthy fingernails. Then I realize I've seen these men before. These are the men who kill me in my vision.

Oh, God.

"Oh, look. She started the party already," the man with the knife says with a smile as he gestures with the blade toward the shard of metal protruding from my shoulder.

The blond smiles at me, releases my wrist, and viciously rips out the shard. My scream of agony is trapped in my throat as he tightens his grip on my neck. My fingers claw at his hand, but he is too strong. His friend's laugh echoes in my ears—the tinny sound fading with each second without air.

I can't breathe... They're going to kill me... I can't... breathe... I can't...

The world starts fading away and I feel guilty. I shouldn't have left Kyle like that. Jerk or not, he'd stayed with me. I should have waited for him.

Just before I black out, the blond starts screaming, and for the life of me, I cannot understand why until I see his sleeve catch fire. My eyes follow the flames from his sleeve to my hand and my brain can't quite seem to grasp what I'm seeing.

My hand is covered in fire—orange and yellow and blue flames licking up my skin like a caress of a lover. I don't feel pain from the fire, in fact, I feel just the opposite. My right shoulder, which just a moment ago was a ball of pure agony, is knitting back together. I feel the blood slowing—the flesh mending on its own.

And my fingers still grip his hand, the flames blackening his skin from their heat. I feel stronger, healthier, and pissed right the fuck off.

When Kyle said Phoenix, he wasn't lying. If I grow a beak, I'm going to be pissed.

The man with the scar is still screaming and the one with the knife doesn't look so smug right about now. But I have to give him credit, he won't leave his friend. He slashes and stabs with that damn knife trying to get me to let go of his burning friend.

And I do. I let him go because he's stopped screaming and is a ball of burning flesh on the ground.

"Why did you do this? Why attack me?" I yell at knife-man. Because seriously. What the fuck did I ever do to them? Not that I'd remember if I had, but shit.

"Whaddya mean, you damn devil? You shoulda known you'd have a bounty on your head. You can't go round killing kids and have no consequences," he replies.

"What?" I breathe. *Killing kids? No. No, I didn't do that. I would never do that. That wasn't me. NO.*

My brain screams at me—telling me his words aren't true, but knife-boy breaks in. My head shakes of its own accord, denying his words.

"Yes, ma'am. You have a bounty on your pretty little head and I aim to collect," he says as he lunges with the knife, and I'm still so stunned at his words I can't defend myself fast enough. The blade pierces my belly to the hilt.

I can't think of anything but the pain. So, I don't hear his screaming as my fire hits his flesh when I grab his arms for support as my legs give out. I don't notice when his screams die. I don't see when he turns to ash just from touching my skin.

Because I have his hunting knife in my gut—pouring my lifeblood into the dying, autumn grass.

My eyes snag on the sky as I fall to my back in the pile of smoldering ashes and bone. I really hope I didn't kill innocent children. I hope Kyle finds us because Max is hurt.

And I hope I sleep without bad dreams.

I really don't want to go back to the dark.

NICOLA—KENTUCKY BEFORE

I never saw him coming.

Just my luck, I suppose, I would find my love when I knew I wasn't long for this world.

Getting a mate before my inevitable end seemed like a horrible thing at first, but I couldn't help the slight niggles of happiness which broke through the wall around my heart.

I'd built that wall myself out of the broken promises and lies told to me in my youth. It kept me safe—staved off the loneliness and heartbreak—but it didn't keep him out.

My visions all but dried up nearly a month ago, but I knew from all the ones before Iva worked the forbidden magic which damned my sight I wasn't going to make it. Three centuries seemed so long and so short all at the same time. How could I have had so much time on this earth and wasted it? Is this what humans feel like when approached with a terminal illness? Do they lament the time they spent on trivial matters and wish they'd done more?

Do they have so much regret?

Everything I'd done, every single atrocity and willful neglect—all of the things I could have prevented, the lives I could have saved—made me the worst sort of person. But I did them all knowing I was saving my race —sure I had dirt under my nails, but all my toils wouldn't be for nothing.

I hoped.

Time was speeding by, and I wanted to experience everything I'd been denied. I wasn't going to feel the perfection of an evil put to death or the purity of wrongs being righted. I wasn't going to see my greatest sin washed from my soul. But I could have a little bit of happiness before I went, and with my plan in place and the first domino about to fall... Time was a luxury I no longer had.

Then, he came along with his hulking presence and soft, rumbling voice and death seemed like a blessing and a curse. A blessing because I hadn't had much happiness in my life and he seemed like a gift given to me at the very last second. But a curse as well because I wasn't going to get to keep him. I didn't deserve him and I never would, and the burn of losing him—even if it was in my own death—seemed hotter than any flame I could produce.

But he didn't need to know, and since my time was coming to a close, he didn't have to. I could flit in and out of his long life and be no more than a blip. Yes. I could do that. I could love him to distraction, lose myself in the beautiful newness of a fleeting love, and no one would be the wiser. Especially him. It would be the one gift I could give myself—a single bit of happiness in a rather difficult and awful life.

I wasn't as limited as I'd let everyone believe. Sure, I'm blind in the most basic of senses, but the beauty of being an Oracle is it didn't matter. I saw so much more with my mind; I didn't need my eyes. But he came after my visions dried up, and of all the things I saw, of all the events I foretold...

I didn't see him, and I should have.

I laid in this enormous bed listening to his soft breathing, listening to the house and the wind in the trees. It was beautiful here. The sounds here were the best. The low rumble of the TV while he puttered around the kitchen, making lunch. The sound of him chopping wood out back for the fireplace. The sound of Kyle humming to himself as he worked on spells to strengthen the warding around his property.

Any of the million sounds I cherished because they were his.

Just last week, he procured a new violin from somewhere, giving me my very first present ever in my life. At first, I was scared to touch it. What if I busted the strings, or dropped it when I stubbed my toe on furniture?

It had been so long since I had to use my senses instead of my abilities. I was clumsy and inept and I couldn't bear to destroy the only present I'd ever been given. But I played it. For him I played my goodbye. He knew the song for what it was, and he was angry with me, but I had to tell him, had to prepare him for this.

I just wished it hadn't come so soon.

I reached across the tiny space between us, knowing a vision would come at any moment. Brushing back a stray lock from Kyle's sleeping face, I relished his visage in my mind's eye. He was so beautiful. It made me smile so hard knowing his outside matched his inside.

Iva must have died—only her first death, I knew—but there was no other explanation for my visions to so suddenly return to me. I didn't think it all would end so quickly. Didn't think I would love him so swiftly or so much. I didn't think it would all hurt so much.

But it did.

I cupped his face and placed a gentle kiss on his lips before removing myself from our bed. No. His bed. This house wasn't ours, that bed wasn't ours, and soon, even he wouldn't be mine.

Because soon I wouldn't be living. Soon, I would have to endure and hold on like Aurelia did, like Mena did. I would have to endure all the horrors of Iva had in store for me, but unlike my cousins, I wouldn't live to tell the tale.

When the vision hit me, sitting at the kitchen table of the house I loved so much, it was so much worse than I thought it would be.

Because I wasn't the only one who would lose.

II

KYLE—AFTER

Nicola is in deep shit. From me certainly, because as soon as I find her, I'm tanning that lily-pale ass. I cannot believe she left me here. She knows absolutely nothing about the world—either worlds. Not this human one, and sure as shit, not the Ethereal. Not the politics, the dangers, fucking nothing. She has no fucking clue, and I swear to everything holy if she gets hurt I'm going to wring her skinny neck.

Goddammit, Shortcake. Where the fuck are you?

Nicola's speeding heartbeat trips in my chest, her adrenaline and fear mixed with a healthy dose of anger filters through me, and for the first time, I realize that the bonding took. I didn't think it would. When I sliced my fangs into her hand, I had no idea if the Wraith bond would even work for us. I'm only half-Wraith for one, and for two…

I wasn't sure there was a soul left inside her to bond to, wasn't sure there was anything left to Nicola at all. I know the emotions I'm feeling are hers and not mine—don't ask me how, I just do. They feel different, foreign and yet not. I feel her, and when we were so close together, I didn't realize I could.

I'm probably going to hell for thinking this, but I'm glad I had the foresight to do it before she could say no. I'm not sorry—not in the least. In my defense, I bound my body and soul to hers when I thought she was dying, figuring I'd follow her like my father followed my mother, like John followed Olivia. I knew when I bound her she might never wake up. She was it for me. Nicola Miller was mine, and if she was leaving this earth, I was going with her, no matter how hard she tried to keep me here alone. I knew then—just like I know now—I won't live in a world without her in it.

Even though she didn't wake up the Nicola I knew, I'm still thankful I did it. Probably more right this very second because it will make finding her that much easier. However, if Aurelia or Mena figure out I bound Nic while she was unconscious, I'm going to get my ass kicked three ways to Sunday.

I feel a pull on my chest, guiding me, yanking me from that room and down the stairwell to the front entrance, through the doors, and to the parking lot. Glad that for once I actually had my truck here, I climb in and crank the engine, peeling out from the lot and hauling ass north. I should call West or Ash for help. I should, but I don't. I have to see if I can find her on my own. I can't intrude on my friends every single time I have a problem—they've already done too much for us, and we've hurt them too much already.

I can't ask them for more.

As soon as I make it to the freeway, I'm hit with a wave of bone deep terror—her heart rate is going through the roof. Shit. I stomp on the gas, praying to anything I can that I get there in time. Nausea roils in my gut as her heart runs double-time in my chest. She's scared, she's hurt. Oh, God.

Please, please, please. I can't lose her.

It takes forever for me to get to the exit—it might have only been a minute, but I'm too far away from her. I can't protect her from here. I don't slow down enough as I take a left at the stoplight and damn near roll the truck as I skid back and forth on the narrow two-lane country road far outside the city limits.

I see the wreck almost immediately, but my mind refuses to process it fully. I scramble from the cab after hastily putting it in park, feeling Nicola's pull, knowing she's nearby.

I study the fused, crumpled hoods of the filthy, mud-covered four-by-four and the cherry red Chevelle. Both of the truck's doors are open wide, the incessant dinging of the door alarm grating on my nerves. The Chevelle's windows are busted, and I find a bloody blue-haired woman passed out in the driver's seat. She smells of Witch and a little of something else I can't place. As I inspect her, I notice the passenger door on the Chevelle is thrown open. Then, the smell of blood, wolf, burnt flesh and bone, and gasoline filters through my shock. Oh, God.

She feels so close. Where the fuck is she?

My eyes snag on something red in the dying grass just beyond the open passenger door, and in the time it takes for me to round the trunk, my brain sluggishly trails behind my heart in figuring out what that red is.

Nicola lays flat on her back in a pile of smoldering ash and bone; her crimson curls spread over the blackened earth. Her breaths are shallow and pained, the blood staining her sweater and the fingers that are pitifully trying to pry the thick hunting knife from her belly.

"Baby," I whisper, shock hitting every vital function of my body as I fall to my knees at her side.

Nicola's eyes sluggishly meet mine. I see the apology in them, the regret, and I do the only thing I can. I pull the phone from the back pocket of my jeans and call for help.

"Crane," Asher's low, groggy voice answers on the fourth ring.

"I-I n-need h-help," I stutter, wondering if I should pull the blade out or leave it in.

Willa said Nic wasn't healing like she should. What if I pull it out and she bleeds out before she can regenerate? What if she dies and doesn't come back?

What if we both die?

"Kyle? Hey, man. Are you okay?" Asher replies, his voice more alert. I hear a rustle of fabric and him whispering to his wife, Mena, to wake up and get dressed.

"Not me. It's N-nicola. We need help. Please, she's hurt. Bring Mena and Ian," I plead, not breaking eye contact with Nicola.

"Where are you?" he barks, ready to help us, no questions asked.

I rattle off something about sending him my location and hang up to send him my coordinates, fumbling with the keys until I get it right.

Grabbing Nic's hand, I gently squeeze it saying, "Help is coming, baby. Help is coming."

"Mm... M-max," she murmurs, her voice a pain-clogged whisper.

"What, babe?"

"Max... Wo-woman. In the car. H-help her. She's hurt. Au-Aurelia sent her to he-help me."

I want to look back to check on this Max, but I can't break Nic's stare. I can't look away from the amber eyes I hated so much just twenty-four hours ago. How could I have hated them? Despite their color, they belong to my Nicola—a woman so preoccupied with saving others that she gets herself hurt.

Dammit, baby, why did you run off like that?

Soon, the grass is crowded with seven pairs of feet, and without looking up I know who they belong to. Mena, Asher, Evan, West, Aidan, Ian and Cam, but all I care about are the two sets that spring into action. The faint sizzle of Mena's gentle touch pulls my eyes away from Nicola's.

"Willa said she's not healing like she supposed to. I didn't know what to do. I don't know what to do..." I murmur, unable to bring my voice any higher.

"Let me see what I can do. Okay, big man?" Mena asks, her naturally calming nature oozing through me even when my whole world is falling apart all over again.

Mena is a different kind of being. Classified as a

Phoenix, she attained the mantle of their leader due to her natural ability as an Aegis. An Aegis cannot be controlled, cannot be contained, and the sheer power coursing underneath her skin is enough raw electricity to blow a hole in the world. Regal in the most organic way, Mena is nearly six feet of willowy badass. Dark hair pulled back into a fighting queue, revealing sharp cheekbones and piercing eyes, Mena could only be classified as beautiful. Beautiful in the deadliest of ways. The only woman I know who could match her is Aurelia—her fraternal twin.

Mena scoots me out of the way and places her hands on Nicola, sharing the natural energy that flows through her. Nic's eyes flutter shut—either from relief or from the pain I don't know which—and I fight with myself not to lose it. I can't lose it on Mena. Ian settles in opposite her and gets to work trying to remove the knife, and then I go black-eyed, ready to rip him apart. Ian Moran is the best medic we have only surpassed by Mena's natural ability, but when he touches the knife in Nic's belly... I can't contain the growl that rips up my throat or the phase that whips over my body.

Shit. He's helping her. Stop it, I think, but my body has other ideas. Ideas that involve blood and fire, talons and teeth.

Two sets of hands pull me to my feet and it is a

struggle to meet West's and Asher's stares. I feel everyone looking at me, I feel their censure. I can't for the life of me figure out what I did wrong, but fuck it. I did what I thought was right.

Asher says nothing, but Ash doesn't talk much anyway. The burly blond man simply stares at me, waiting for me to explain. West has no such need for silence.

"We couldn't get a call before the shit hit the fan? When did she wake up?" West asks, arms crossed.

West Carmichael is a big man, not quite six and a half feet, and almost as broad as I am. Hair reaching his shoulders when it isn't up in a topknot for fighting, tattoos reaching from neck to ankle and thick gauges in his ears, the only thing we have in common physically is our black hair and beards. But what I have over him in height and muscle mass, he makes up in power. Our newly minted King used to be the former King's assassin, and in his tenure, West has wiped out countless threats to our way of life. He can kill someone faster than I can blink, and he is not pleased.

Sure, he's my oldest friend and technically my King, but honestly, I wasn't sure Nicola would be welcome in my circle of friends. She did have an evil bitch from hell literally inhabiting her body. The things I saw Iva do with Nicola's body still make me shudder.

And I know the difference. Everyone might not be so sympathetic.

"We hit some snags," is all I reply with.

The shrug that accompanies my less-than-forthcoming reply is just asking for an ass-kicking. It comes in the form of a tiny, pixie fist in my gut. No one that small should pack as much power as Evan does.

Evangeline Black (or it could be Carmichael now, for all I know) is five feet tall at a push. With curly pale blonde hair and bright blue eyes, she is deceptively sweet-looking, a fact she uses in her favor. Evangeline is one of the deadliest women I have ever met, and she doesn't need a weapon in her hand—she is a weapon. San Francisco earthquake of 1906 ring a bell? That was her, and she was only twenty-one then.

Evan doesn't even look at me, her eyes only on Nic and I find I'm more worried about what she'll do to Nicola than I should be for my own hide. Her hand resting on the hilt of the lethal tri-dagger sheathed at the belt of her fighting leathers eases my concerns exactly zero.

"What kind of snags?" Cam asks, and I notice the surly man for the first time. Shit. I need to get my fucking head together. Cameron O'Connor is a Guardian to the last Wraith royal family—Evangeline and West to be exact—staking his life against his ability to keep them breathing.

"She has absolutely no idea who she is, who we are, or what happened. She didn't even know what she was," I explain, side-eyeing my Queen so I don't get another sock in the gut.

"I'd say she does now. Is that char-broiled Wolf I smell?" Aidan asks with a semi-suppressed shudder, the Guardian looking visibly ill.

"Yep. Willa said there were wolves at the boundary. We were going to be kicked out when Nic got a vision of us dying. Nic... she left to save me."

"Is there a reason I smell Witch?" Aidan asks, and it reminds me there is an unconscious woman that needs attention.

"Oh! Yeah. There's a woman passed out in the driver's seat. Nic said Aurelia sent her to help."

"Of course she did," Mena pipes in while she finishes up a field dressing.

"She got a name?" Ian asks as he hoists his med bag and rounds the pile of ash and bone to get to the open passenger door.

"Yeah. Nic said it was Max?"

"Max? Aurelia's Max?" Evan asks.

"Guess so," I reply with a shrug.

"Well, assess her injuries and take her with us. We

need to move and if Ari sent her we'll need her help,"
Mena instructs knowing her twin's wishes even though
she is across the world. "Kyle, Nicola needs surgery—
Ian and I can do it in the med bay in my house, or we
can take her back to the Knoxville hospital. I'd rather
take her with us, but it's up to you."

It's a no-brainer for me. As much as Willa thinks
that hospital is a safe place, I don't trust it. It is solely
Witch ran, and to kick us out into a war is a bullshit
quality for people who claim to be neutral.

I want to say we'll go with them, but I don't get to
answer Mena's question. Nicola's eyes flash open,
illuminated with a vision strong enough to bow her
broken body off of the ground with the force of it. It
takes both Mena and me together to keep her down.

And she's screaming...

The sound coming out of her mouth has its own
talons and teeth. It speaks of terror and agony and fear.
But I don't need her to tell me what's coming. I can
smell it on the cool, autumn Tennessee wind.

Wolves.

12

KYLE—AFTER

ALL I'VE EVER ASKED FOR IN MY LIFE WAS PEACE. AS A CHILD I had it, but after my parents left this world, peace has been hard to come by. I keep to myself. I find things that need to be found. I live a quiet life—or at least I did before Nic came into it.

Now look at us.

The glow of eyes from the wolves surrounding our small circle is enough for me to know we don't have enough weapons. Having Mena here isn't enough. Having Evangeline here isn't enough. We aren't enough.

Aidan and Cam draw heavy swords from the scabbards at their belts.

"No one said wolves. A wolf problem heads up

would have been a good thing to give before we came. What the shit, Ky?" Aidan grouches.

He's right. Wolves are—for lack of a better word—a whole other animal. Shifters are neutral—usually benign. Wolves are more times than not, a feral, pissed-off race of hooligans and mountain and swamp people. They steal, they pilfer, and they are fucking shifty. Nothing against mountain or swamp people, but wolves give them a bad name. Every wolf I've ever met has had several screws loose and is half a step shy of full-blown bat-shit crazy.

One is a problem. A whole pack like this?

We are fucked and not in a good way.

Aidan and Cam are ready to fight—the dumb bastards. West and Asher are smarter and look for an exit strategy. Evan is having none of it.

"We've got to go!" Evan orders as she bends to grab Nicola's arm—the black smoke of her travel has her taking my woman from me in an instant.

"Goddammit!" West and I say at the same time. Pissed off she left without them, Cam, Aidan and West follow her.

I turn to grab Max, knowing Ian isn't able to travel due to his particular cocktail of mixed heritage, but his answering growl is more feral than the wolves ready to attack.

And another one bites the dust.

I wish I could tell him to wait—to not pull that thread—but he wouldn't listen to me, so I'll save my breath. He'll have to figure it out on his own just like I did—just like I'm still trying.

I look back to Mena and Asher and nod for them to go. The roar of running feet hits my ears, and I know we have exactly zero time before they are on us.

"We don't have time for this shit. I'll take you both," I mutter, snatching Max's wrist before Ian can take a chunk out of me. Grabbing the back of his neck, I pull them both with me as I get us the fuck out of there.

As soon as the porch steps of Asher and Mena's Colorado mountain home are under my feet, Max's still-unconscious body is ripped from my grasp by a growling Ian.

"What the fuck, man?" I mutter, raising my hands in surrender as I leave him in the dust, climbing the rest of the steps to get to Nicola. I do not have the time or inclination to deal with that bullshit.

I have enough problems.

"You bonded her, didn't you," a voice I didn't expect to hear calls from the living room.

I turn to see Aurelia seated in the corner rocking chair, a dark-haired baby asleep on her chest. I can't tell if it is Henry or Livvy—her four-month-old twins—but it doesn't matter. The child on her chest prevents her from launching herself across the room to kick my ass. Aurelia Constantine—like Mena—has Aegis blood. Classified as a Phoenix and cursed with the sight, Aurelia knows so much more than she lets on, possesses carefully honed fighting abilities and knows what moves you'll make before you decide to make them. Fighting her is just begging to bleed, and she'll make sure you do with a smile on her face.

"You see, I know for certain I asked you when we started this mess if you'd bonded her and you said no. So that means you had to have done it when she couldn't answer you. You had to have done it when she was in a fucking coma, Kyle," her low voice murmurs in the dim. "Please tell me why I shouldn't kick your ass up and down this mountain. Because I'm drawing a blank."

Aurelia's pale, pupilless eyes focus on me—which to this day is fucking frightening—and I see what she won't say. She's scared for Nicola and for me, and no matter what she says, she's scared she'll lose both of us.

"She going to make it?" the question falls brokenly from my lips. I don't want to ask. I don't want to know if she's not.

"Yep. Whether the both of you make it out of this, though..." she says, shrugging a single shoulder so the baby on her chest isn't disturbed. "I could never see as far ahead as Nicola could. Now, go wash your hands and come back to hold Livvy so I can get something to eat."

I know I don't have the option of telling her no. As one of the two living relatives that Nicola has, staying on her good side is pretty much my only choice. I stomp into the kitchen, and flip on the tap, and it is only when I watch the water turn red do I realize how much of Nicola's blood is on my hands.

I feel like I am about to crack—like everything that makes me sane is slowly circling the drain along with Nicola's blood. It is so hard to watch the water run clear, as if I'm losing another piece of us all over again. I finally sack up and turn off the tap, drying my hands on a nearby dish towel. When the rag comes away red again, I notice Nic's blood is on my hoodie as well.

Fuck.

Stripping off the sweatshirt until I'm down to the thin, white t-shirt underneath, I hold onto my phase by the skin of my teeth. Shit, I damn near tear out my own hair trying not to rip the room apart.

All that blood...

Aurelia clears her throat to get my attention, motioning me over to take her seat, putting a sleeping Livvy in my arms once I'm settled in the thick upholstered rocking chair. Livvy doesn't stir—even in the transfer to my awkward arms, her delicate rosebud mouth a perfect little 'o' of a passed out baby.

"You're keeping me from the med bay so I don't rip anyone apart, aren't you?"

"And doubling down with a sleeping baby so you have to stay calm. I'm practically diabolical," she deadpans.

Turning to leave me alone with her daughter, Aurelia stops in her tracks when she crosses the open front door. Arms crossed and mouth pursed in a disapproving pout, she taps her dainty, ballet flat shod foot on the hardwood for a second. I have no idea what she's looking at, but whatever or whoever they are, are about to get it.

That's when I hear it. I didn't notice it before, but I would venture a guess that Max is awake—especially when Aurelia takes a huge step back from the open door just as Ian sails through it. Wrapped in a thick mist of green magic, Ian is thrown over the threshold, landing face-first on the foyer tile with a crash.

Livvy stirs in my arms, but settles down when I start rocking the chair again, patting her baby booty as I lift her to my shoulder. She nuzzles into my neck and I swear I didn't think I could be as protective over this tiny person as I am right this second. It makes me wonder when—or if—Nic and I will have kids. Will they have her fiery red hair? Her pale skin? Will they take after me?

Will Nic ever remember us before all this shit happened? Will she ever want me like that again?

I pat Livvy's back again, gently holding this little beacon of life to me. Max stalks through the door, ready to kick Ian's ass, but my growl stops her. If she wakes this baby up, I'm going to be really fucking pissed off.

Max is a sight with her blue hair unraveled from her carefully pinned victory rolls, blood half covering her face and neck, and green magic sparking from her fingertips. Her cropped leather jacket, blood-stained jeans and bright red heels only highlight how deadly she looks.

"Max, honey. Why are you trying to kill Ian?" Aurelia asks, drawing Max's eye for the first time. The anger on her face fades to confusion and then to chagrin.

"He's not a wolf, is he?" Max says as she points to Ian's sprawled and slightly stunned body.

"Nope," Aurelia answers and I shake my head to confirm when she looks to me.

"Huh. Sorry, dude, I don't know. You caught me rather unawares," she shrugs addressing Ian. "Umm. Speaking of unaware, where am I? Where's my car? And most importantly, what the fuck happened and why am I bleeding?" she says as she looks down at herself.

The magic dies from her fingertips as she inspects her blood-covered hand. The caramel skin of her face turns white in an instant and Ian is up and to her before anyone else can move, catching her as her legs give way. Ian hoists her up into his arms, and stalks out of the room to what I assume is the med bay, leaving Aurelia and I alone in the living room once again.

"Where's Rhys?" I ask.

"Getting Henry to sleep upstairs," Aurelia answers as she stares after Max and Ian, her eyes aglow.

"When did you get back?"

"About fifteen minutes ago. Would have been here sooner, but the plane had to refuel in Houston," she says yawning.

"Sorry you had to come back to this."

"Meh. Taking a honeymoon was a longshot anyway. There's too much shit going on. We had a good day at the beach with the kids. It was good enough for me."

"You didn't need food, did you?"

"Nope. It was a ruse to make you hold my Phoenix spawn," she replies, batting her eyelashes at me.

"You are so weird," I chuckle

"Thank you. Isn't it a rule that your in-laws have to be bat shit crazy? I mean, come on. I'm doing my civic duty here to keep with tradition. You should be thanking me. It's not like any of us have a mother in law to annoy the shit out of us. Cousins will just have to do."

Family who won't leave you hanging even when the world falls apart? If this is the only family we have, family made from friends and blood and loyalty?

I'll take it and be happy.

13

NICOLA—TENNESSEE BEFORE

If I never heard the sound of Kyle's screams it would've been too soon. They floated to me on torn wings of sound from the chamber at the end of the hall. Stuck in this stone tomb of a prison, I knew I wouldn't make it out of here. This was the place I would die—or at least the god forsaken torture room was.

I didn't want this. Not then. Not ever. Had I known Kyle would have been caught up in this mess, I wouldn't have gone with him that day back in July. I would have done anything—sacrificed anything—to keep this from him. I did everything they wanted. I acted like everything was fine. I made excuses... but they hurt him anyway. I'd only been here for a week, but Kyle? He'd been in the god forsaken hell hole this whole fucking time. A month I'd been dodging my cousins, meting out the orders so he wouldn't be hurt, but by the time I got here I saw how much they'd already done to him.

It wasn't fair. I did everything they asked!

Kyle's screams echoed through me again—their awful guttural bellows ripping up my insides as I tried to find the strength to ignore them. I didn't have it. I couldn't do this anymore. I couldn't let this happen anymore. Not to him.

He didn't deserve this. He didn't deserve the pain loving me brought him. He didn't earn this evil.

Kyle was good and right and everything I wasn't. He was worthy of loving. I wasn't worth the dirt on his boot. Not after the cards I'd dealt. Not after what I'd done just to get to this very spot. I had to quit stalling. It was only causing him more pain.

I'd made up my mind by the time he came for me that I would do whatever Devereux asked of me.

Devereux shouldn't be alive. I felt it whenever he came near. There was something wrong with his soul. He felt wrong, shredded—almost as if what made him a person was gone. This didn't surprise me even a little bit. Devereux Emerson died over a century ago keeping

Evangeline alive—whatever this thing was—it couldn't really be him.

Could it?

The door to my cell swung wide and Devereux's hard fist made itself at home against my temple, and it was lights out for me for a long while.

Waking up in a new place frightened me. It was so difficult to orient myself in a room I didn't walk first. There were new smells, new sounds, but this wasn't a new place. If my shackles were anything to go by, I knew exactly where we were. I also knew without a shred of doubt that my time was up.

Devereux's footsteps made their way towards me. They sounded so different from anyone else's—not plodding, not heavy, just a whisper soft menace that turned my stomach.

Devereux's breath hit my ear, and if that wasn't enough to incite a full-body shudder, his words surely did the trick. What he wanted I couldn't give him. No one could.

"I'm bringing Iva back, Nikki. And you're going to help me. I'm going to put my mistress into this lush little body of yours, and then we're going to have so much fun."

I tried to get away—to scramble off that table—but

my bonds held me close to the scarred wood. I couldn't agree to this—I couldn't let this be it.

Not me. Not this.

So horrified I couldn't possibly utter a single sound, I shook my head—denying his words, denying that this was what was meant for me.

He didn't like my answer and I heard a blade cutting, cutting, cutting and his voice...

No, please don't make me do this.

"Come on, Nikki. Tell me. The lung? The heart? Maybe the liver? How do you want your mate to die, Nikki? How painful do you want it to be? Say yes, and I'll let him go. Say no one more time, and I'll make his death last days."

Devereux wasn't a patient man and before I could do or say anything, he did something to Kyle. Kyle's indrawn breath laced with pain made me change my answer.

If it meant he'd live, if it meant he'd go free, I would do anything, endure anything. For him I would.

"No, Nic. Don't do this. Don't let them do that to you," Kyle pleaded, his voice slurred with a drug or spell, maybe both. The yank at his manacles, his futile tries to break free, slapped at me. He had to live.

He had to.

"I have to. There's no other way," I said as I choked on my tears, begging for him to understand.

This was my last good thing. The only really good thing I would ever do. Because it didn't fall into a caveat of a vision or a plan. It wasn't a chess move. I did this only because I loved him.

I wanted him to live.

Even if I wouldn't be around to see it.

NICOLA—AFTER

I fight for consciousness, clawing my way out of the blackness that holds me so tight. The room I wake up in appears to be a guest room in a homey but elegant house. Walls painted a warm cream, sunlight streams in through the blinds and dances off the sheen of a gilt-framed mirror on an adjacent wall. A tall dresser, stained a rich walnut, rests against the west wall, a pitcher of wildflower resting on top.

I don't wake up in a hospital. Not a dungeon. Not a shanty filled with wolves. Just a comfortable bed, in a beautiful room, on a sunny morning. It feels too good to be true. More so, when Kyle walks in from the adjoining bathroom, shirtless with a towel wrapped around his waist, another towel in his hands rubbing the water from his hair.

Yep. Definitely dreaming.

The honeyed caramel of his skin reaches far and wide over the thick delineated muscles of his chest and abs. This isn't the body of a boy, that's for damn sure. Kyle's chest is only marginally marred by the pale crisscrossing of old scars, but across his stomach is the freshly healed pink of a large new one.

I wonder what did that to him, and I hope whoever it was, died bloody.

Kyle doesn't notice my ogling; he just continues across the room, drying his hair as he pulls open the top drawer of the dresser and fishes out a pair of plain black boxer briefs. I can't make myself turn away as he drops his towel and bends to pull them on.

Now, I'm not exactly sure about the rest of the planet—I feel like I was born yesterday—but his ass has to beat every other one out there. Wide shoulders jam-packed with muscles tapering down to a narrow waist, firm, round globes of the best ass on the planet, and thick corded thighs. I won the lottery, didn't I, I think as my sex clenches. Whoa, this man is potent.

I should feel guilty for staring, right? I don't, but I should. Probably? Maybe? No. I shouldn't feel guilty for admiring a man who is my husband. Isn't that written in the marriage bylaws? Thou shalt ogle your spouse.

I can't help myself, I give him a long wolf whistle.

Kyle startles, jumping to standing, unfortunately bringing those boxer briefs up and over his very delectable ass and what I can bet is a substantial piece of equipment.

The laugh that breaks from me feels good—for about three seconds—until the pain finally reaches my brain and I remember I took a knife to the gut.

Holy fucking God. I'm never laughing again.

"Don't say that, Shortcake. You'll heal up in no time, and I'll get you laughing again," Kyle murmurs in my ear as he slips into bed next to me and gathers me close. His warmth seeps through my pain and eases the fire in my poor abused muscles. I feel comfortable there in his arms - like I've been gone too long and am finally heading home.

"Glad to know you like what you see, though," he teases and I feel the skin of my cheeks heat with what I can only guess is a beet-red blush.

"Don't get a big head, I just couldn't believe how bloody big you are. What are you, half-Sasquatch?"

Half something, I could swear he mumbles, and at my confused look, he slips from the bed and pulls on a pair of jeans lying across a plush, pale gray corner chair.

I wish he wouldn't leave.

Now that the pain has fully woken me up, things are coming back to me, and the questions in my head outnumber the things I know. How did he find me? How did I get here? Where am I? Are we safe? Is he safe?

I open my mouth to voice all my concerns but snap it shut again. I can't keep taking. I can't keep being selfish. Never again. When I part my lips for the second time, it is to issue the apology he deserves.

"I'm sorry," I say, my voice clogged with the tears I refuse to shed.

"For what, Shortcake? As far as I know, you didn't do anything wrong," he says frowning.

"I shouldn't have left without you. I don't know how you found us, but I'm glad you did. I'd likely be dead if you hadn't."

Confusion puckers his brow, and I feel like I may have said something wrong.

"Shortcake, that knife wouldn't have been able to kill you. A car wreck can't kill you. Hell, a bomb can't kill you. If I broke your neck right now, you'd wake up in a week ready to kick my ass. Very few things can scar you, and as far as I know, only two things can take your life. Out of the two of us, you are more indestructible than I am."

"So why did it feel like I was dying?"

"Because, in a sense, you were. A Phoenix regenerates perpetually. You don't age and never will. The only thing that can kill you is a Morganite blade or an Aegis. That's it. Now, me on the other hand... Because we are bonded, I'm not sure how exactly it works. I'd have to ask Mena."

Interesting. "Wrapping my brain around all of this might take some time."

"Well, that's one thing you have plenty of, Shortcake."

I guess so.

14

NICOLA—AFTER

Being laid up in bed is probably my least favorite thing. It's been six hours, and I hate it. The first hour I could have taken it, but being unable to walk to the bathroom by myself or fetch myself something to eat grates on me. I don't like relying on anyone—even if the man I'm relying on is a six foot seven bearded powerhouse who speaks to me in the gentlest of tones.

But I hadn't seen anyone in hours—three to be exact if the old-school alarm clock was anything to go by. Kyle didn't come back to my—our—room and I was getting worried. I swing my pajama-clad legs over the side of the bed. Three hours ago, I couldn't move my legs at all.

Mena said it was because the blade nicked my spinal cord.

Mena Constantine. Kyle told me she is my cousin, but I see zero resemblance between us. She towers over me at nearly six feet tall, her skin the color of warm caramel, and her hair almost black for how dark it is. I don't exactly look anything like her with my red hair, pale skin, and amber eyes.

She seemed nice enough, but I felt like I was missing a whole slew of information. I felt as if I should know her, but couldn't quite place her face. I felt at a disadvantage, and after the last few days of not knowing anyone or anything, I felt uncomfortable being here in this house where everyone knew me, and I didn't know them.

Just as I find my feet—something Mena said would be coming along within the next day—my door opens wide. A woman stands in the middle of it, a tray of food in her hands. Raven black hair pulled into a messy bun on top of her head, caramel skin beautifully decorated with vibrantly colored ink beneath her short-sleeved top, and what looks like a baby strapped to her chest in a turquoise baby carrier. But her eyes are what gives me pause—pale, pupilless green with enough zing to them that I know for sure she isn't blind. Even with the apprehension they give me, she's still a woman with her hands full.

"Let me help you," I say as I cross the few feet to her on trembling legs, taking the tray from her and setting it on the cedar chest at the foot of the bed. It is laden down with a grilled cheese sandwich made from two thick slabs of bread and oozing a beautiful orange cheddar. Next to the sandwich is a fragrant bowl of what appears to be chicken tortilla soup, a bottle of water, and a fan of apple slices.

"Thanks. I figured you were hungry," she says, holding out a hand to shake. I take it and feel a minor frisson of electricity snake up my arm from her touch.

"Aurelia?" I guess only because Mena has a more potent version of the same handshake.

"Yep, and this little monster is Henry," she says, pointing to the dark head sleeping on her chest as she drops a kiss to his forehead.

"He's beautiful." And he is. Black eyelashes sweep his beautifully chubby cheeks, his mouth in a tiny baby pout of reluctant sleep.

"He's a menace, but you're right, he is beautiful. The little heathen didn't want to nap and shocked the shit out of Rhys. His toddler years are going to be a fucking joy, that's for sure. Plus, I figured he would make me seem less threatening. Mena says I can be abrasive," she explains.

I can't necessarily say it was a bad call. Small as she may be, her presence is formidable to the point of intimidating.

"I'm happy to meet you and Mr. Henry. I am so sorry to impose on you. Max said it was your honeymoon and I just feel awful bringing this mess to your doorstep. I appreciate everyone's willingness to help us out."

Aurelia looks at me with confusion, a single eyebrow raised.

"What?" I ask.

"I can't recall you ever apologizing for anything ever, Nic. It's weird."

"Why? Was I an asshole before?" I ask, but this doesn't surprise me. The way a few people I've seen look at me, I must have been a first-rate jackass. Either that or I must have done them a great injustice.

"Yes, and I don't think I've ever heard you cuss either."

"Well, Kyle says I'm different now. Considering according to you I was an unapologetic asshole before; I can't say that's a bad thing. Now, I must dig into this delicious spread you brought me. Maybe you can stay and fill me in on yourself. Max said we were family?" I ask, and I do want to know, but my quip about being starved isn't quite on the mark. Standing is taking it out of me faster than I thought it would.

"Of course. Just slip back in bed, and I'll set you up," she says seeing through my claim of hunger.

"Busted, huh?" I ask as I slip back under the covers and she places the tray on my lap.

"Yep. You can't fool a Seer," she says as she moves to sit in the comfy side chair.

"Oh, I don't know about that. I'm getting fooled all the time. I have no clue what's going on."

I pick up the thick sandwich, taking a monster of a bite and groaning at the buttery, cheesy flavor.

"You'll get there. You're still healing, and from what you went through, I'm amazed you're doing as well as you are."

Something tells me she doesn't just mean the wolves. She means before I woke up in the hospital, before I lost my memory and my mind. Before all of this. The newly swallowed bite almost turns sour in my stomach at the thought.

"I don't know what happened to me, so I'll just have to take your word for it. The old noodle isn't exactly what it used to be."

"Didn't anyone—didn't Kyle—tell you?" she asks, her voice a low growl of pissed off woman.

At this point, I decide to be flattered at her ire on my

behalf instead of the fear I probably should feel seeing anger on this formidable woman—baby strapped to her chest or not.

"He tried, I think, but I had a mental breakdown when a certain name was said. I believe he's trying to give me time to either get comfortable with my skin or get my memory back, so he doesn't have to. I kind of feel sorry for the guy. Who would want an amnesiac for a wife?" I ask shrugging as my worry burns a hole in my belly and makes the bite in my tummy turn to ash.

I don't know how much Kyle had to sacrifice or what he endured, but I know it was more than I'm worth. It is a debt I cannot repay.

But I will endeavor to try.

With one look at her, I know Aurelia sees my inadequacies, she sees my guilt, and I don't know how to fix what is wrong with me or how to apologize for whatever I did that I don't remember.

"It is awful being the reason someone is in pain, trust me, I know from experience. The best advice I can give you, is to be honest with him. About your fears, your questions, everything. Trust him to want the best for you—because he does."

"I am the reason, aren't I? So much for wanting to save him."

"Sometimes the sacrifices we make don't always pan out like we thought."

Well that is for damn certain.

"No more running off on your own. No matter the reason. You would have wished for death if I hadn't sent Max to you. You don't have to agree with Kyle. Hell, you don't even have to be nice all the time. But be honest, cousin. Because right now, anything you see, anything you feel is important to the people around you. It is important to keep you safe—to keep us all safe. Don't keep it to yourself. I learned that a long time ago."

KYLE DIDN'T COME BACK. NOT AFTER I FORCED MYSELF TO finish the meal Aurelia brought me or once the night finally fell on the mountains.

I stewed, and I worried over his absence, but he didn't come back to me.

Guess this time I should go to him.

15

KYLE—BEFORE

I wanted to see her one more time before I went to do the one thing I never, ever wanted to do. Before I took everything I loved and threw it away. Before I turned her in.

Tracking has always been my profession. I can find anything and anyone, and with the right spell, I can find them anywhere in this world. Sometimes even in the next.

But finding Nicola's body was harder than it should have been. It took me a long time to heal, a long time before my abilities and my mind cleared enough so my pain didn't taint the spells, and a long time for me to realize that no matter where Nic's body was, this wasn't Nicola.

This was Iva.

Iva was wearing Nic's skin, animating her limbs, and calling the shots. *Iva* was letting that soulless piece of shit Devereux put his hands all over my woman's body. *Iva* was strutting down the streets of the French Quarter with that fucker, letting him touch her skin, letting him put his mouth on her, letting him… I couldn't even finish the thought. And *Iva* was the one doing unthinkable things to innocent children—stealing souls and abilities to fuel her vengeance.

I'd followed her all over this stupid country. To the Oregon wilderness, the barren Arizona desert, the foothills of the Appalachians, and down in the bayous of Louisiana—just missing her in some occasions and others…

Others I just wished I had.

I shouldn't have to see this—no one should have to see someone they love used this way. But I couldn't stay silent and watch anymore. I couldn't let this demon of a woman hurt anyone else. I couldn't let this go on without being a monster myself. Inaction at this point would make me more of a monster than they were.

Not after this. My eyes scanned the once opulent room of a mansion that was now in condemned disrepair. It was tough to tell what filth had been here before, and what was the detritus of spells no one in their right mind would perform.

Wormwood, grave dirt, wolf's bane, pine straw. Nothing but bad things came from those ingredients thrown together.

The black of dried blood mixed with the dirt and silt left over from flood waters that had long since receded was only broken up by the thick white chalk of sigils marked into the crumbling floorboards. Thick wallpaper peeled from the ancient plaster walls, the ceiling missing in some places, and the smell.

Mildew, swamp, fear, death and all the bodily functions that went along with it. I couldn't take it.

I couldn't take the sight of the body I found. A girl— a wolf girl—no more than four years old. Her little body broken well past the repair a phase would give her, her throat mostly torn out, her chest broken open and her heart missing. Blood from her wounds stained her white-blonde hair red and the sight of it reminded me of Nicola's curls so much it physically hurt to look at her.

Wolf females were rare. Hell, wolf children as a whole were rare—so much so it was lucky they hadn't died out centuries ago. What the hell could they want with such a child? Stealing power, I get, but the motives behind this one didn't make any sense. Wolves don't have much power—never had. Of the shifters, wolves have the least political power, and the least territory. One thing—hell the only thing—they had was brute strength, but as crazy as they were, they didn't use it much unless provoked.

There didn't seem to be a rhyme or reason to it, and the brutality. In my long life I'd never seen things like this. Torture, yes, but not mutilation and murder to this level. And children? Never this.

Looking at that house and the poor, broken body of that child brought home all the truths I'd been denying for way too long. I couldn't let Iva squat in Nicola's body. I couldn't let her do this in her skin. I couldn't let Iva's evil taint the body of my woman any more.

I had to be the one to end it. But before I could do that, I had to find her.

For the last time.

KYLE—AFTER

I need to hit something—a face, a wall, anything. I just slipped into bed with her, let her warmth wrap around me and I forgot she doesn't remember me. Her half-Sasquatch comment cemented that fact.

She doesn't remember I'm half-Witch. She doesn't

remember the first time we made love. She doesn't remember what she sacrificed or what Iva did while wearing her skin. She doesn't know what Iva herself did to me. She has no idea and I don't want to be the one to tell her.

So I did what I do best. I left her there in that room to heal up while I scoured the house for a dojo or a workout room or something so I didn't start ripping apart furniture. I found myself in the living room wondering how mad Mena would be if I ripped apart an overstuffed armchair with my talons.

"I have a bone to pick with you," Mena calls from the kitchen, her back to me as she kneads bread at the counter. What is with the Constantine women and cooking all the goddamn time?

"What did I do now?" I ask, flippant when I probably shouldn't be.

"You're lucky I have flour all over my hands, dipshit, or I'd illustrate just how pissed off I am. Sit your big ass down," she scolds, her back still to me.

Deciding it was better to sit than risk my hide, I pull a barstool away from the island and plunk down, crossing my arms in defiance.

"I saw the scar on Nicola's hand. Did you or did you not bind her, Ky?" she asks, but it isn't a question so much as a threat. She already knows the answer; she just wants to see if I'll admit it.

I'm not ashamed of what I did. I'd do it again.

"I did."

"Did you actually ask her, or did you just do it on your own? I'd venture a guess you bit her when she couldn't answer you. Why else would she have a bite on her hand instead of her neck?" she asks, finally looking up at me, her eyes flicking back and forth between green and amber.

"I did it while she was unconscious. I did it when I thought she would either die or never wake up. I would have spent the rest of my life sitting in that hospital chair waiting for her. So you can be pissed at me all you like, I'm still not sorry."

Defiance suits me best, so I stick with it, unapologetically staring her down. If I hadn't held her eyes, I wouldn't know how worried she is.

"What happens when she never remembers? What if this Nicola never loves you? What then?" she asks softly.

I hate that she asks this. I hate that she takes the one fucking thing I'm insecure about and needles it until I want to punch a hole in every single wall I can find.

"Then I have the rest of forever to change her mind.

Either way, she's still mine," my voice a rumble of possession.

"Good answer. Whether you deliver on it remains to be seen."

"I aim to please," I growl through gritted teeth, rising from the stool and heading for the door. I couldn't take the questions swirling in my head any more than I could take the walls and roof of that house.

I had to get out of there. The guilt of leaving would just have to come with me.

16

NICOLA—AFTER

THE TREK DOWN THE WIDE, CURVED STAIRCASE WAS TRICKY. My legs, which were still shaky, wanted nothing more than to give out on me, and my feet kept catching on the plush patterned runner affixed to the middle of the stairs. The house felt empty, but I didn't know if it actually was or if it was my own loneliness and fear coming to bite me in the ass. I clung to the polished walnut handrail for all I was worth, white-knuckling it until my bare feet met the cool hardwood of what I guessed was a great room.

The great room was done up in creams and blues— blues of all shades. A dark cerulean couch mixed with cream and white Moroccan tile patterned throw pillows. A beige, plush armchair sat in the corner with a turquoise throw blanket draped over an arm, and on every single wall not broken up by windows there were shelves and shelves of books filled almost to bursting.

The house was enormous, and the vaulted ceilings and wide windows filled with the blackness of full nightfall only highlighted it. It also highlighted the emptiness in my chest—the fear I felt at being alone again. Call it co-dependent if you want to, but I felt at even more of a disadvantage than anyone rightfully should without Kyle.

I check the kitchen, my gait slow as molasses. No matter how grateful I am that I can actually walk, I'm still irritated with myself.

Sitting at the dining table is a man I haven't met yet.

How many people are in this house?

It isn't until I'm actually faced with another person do I rethink my wardrobe. I glance down at the midnight blue pajama pants and matching camisole top. I feel underdressed and long for an actual bra instead of the shelf thingie Aurelia said was a joke for large breasted women such as ourselves.

She wasn't lying.

The man is tall, not as tall as Kyle, but then not many people are. His skin is a deep tan, and with his Roman nose and dark hair, I feel practically transparent by comparison. His long, lean body is folded into the chair, and hunched over a plate of food, shoveling forkfuls of roast beef and potatoes into his mouth. He gives me a side eye as he goes back to his plate, ignoring me completely. I make it as far as the island barstools before I have to rest, my legs nearly giving out on me.

Silence stretches between us and I feel more and more awkward as I sit waiting for him to say something, anything. I finally give up, breaking the silence.

"What's your name?" I ask, giving him a list of people I've met so far. "I've met Mena, Aurelia and Ian already, but if we've met before, I don't seem to remember."

"We've met," he replies gruffly around his food.

Oh-kay. Obviously I've done something to offend his delicate sensibilities. The delicious smell of spiced meat wafts from the crockpot on the counter. I gingerly slip from the stool and point myself in the direction of filling my belly. The awkwardness not deterring my appetite at all.

"You have some goddamn nerve coming here," his deep voice calls as I grab a plate to dish up the roast.

"I didn't *ask* to come here. No offense, but I have no idea who you are, and since you haven't introduced yourself, I still don't—not that I'd remember you if you did," I reply, turning to face off against the man, plate in hand.

"Like I'd believe a word out of your mouth," he says, pulling himself to standing.

"I'm sorry? Have I offended you in some way?"

"Have you offended me? You've more than fucking offended me. I don't believe you can't remember three hundred some-odd years of chess moves, double dealings, and broken promises, Nicola. Not for one fucking second," he replies, crossing his arms.

I wish I could say I could keep my cool, but I can't.

"You have no idea. You have no idea. You have no fucking idea!" I scream, slamming the porcelain plate down on the stone countertop, smashing it to bits. I'm unable to handle his ire and I lose the tenuous hold I had on my emotions.

"You don't know what it's like to wake up with nothing—no memory, no inkling of anything but the blank space where it used to be. You don't know what it's like to wake up knowing something horrible happened, to know you were the cause, but not know why. To know death is coming for a man you just met, who sat with you every single day you were asleep, who stayed and protected you, and know it's your fault, but can't remember what started it. To have men come after you for a crime you can't remember committing. To hear inklings of how horrible the crime was, and pray to everything holy that it isn't true. You don't know," I growl through gritted teeth, "Don't pretend like you know the first fucking thing about me."

"Iva's sins are hers, but you had sins of your own, Nicola. You may not remember them, but that doesn't erase them," he fires back, and his arrow hits the mark on two fronts.

Just saying that name turns my stomach, causing my breath the speed and my heart to decide it wants to race right on out of my chest. That name makes me want to claw my skin off and douse myself in bleach.

But he's right.

My racing heart gives way to the hollow feeling in my chest—the one I tried to deny—and it hits me threefold. I have the luxury of forgetting. He does not.

"Oh, get the fuck over it, Rhys," Aurelia's voice filters in from the living room, and she stomps into the kitchen in the middle of our standoff.

"It was over a damn century ago, she probably did it to save us, and it has kept me from killing you roughly a thousand times. You should be counting your lucky fucking stars she bound us that way in the first place. Now, Livvy needs a change and Henry is being fussy. You go help Evan deal with the gruesome twosome or I might cut myself on purpose just to teach your dumb ass a lesson," she scolds, hands on her hips, and looking like she is three seconds away from throwing down.

Rhys gives her a decidedly grumpy look, and stalks around the island, getting in her space quick enough to plant a kiss on her lips.

"It really kept you from killing me?" he whispers his question, but it doesn't stop me from hearing it.

"How many times have I actually killed you?"

"It's in the hundreds by now," he replies good naturedly, his voice so much smoother now that he's talking to anyone but me.

"And that was when I knew it would hurt me. What's that tell you, dummy?" she asks and swats him on the butt, effectively shooing him from the room.

Rhys looks back, his expression almost apologetic, but not quite meeting the mark. He still doesn't know what to make of me, and at this point I can't blame him.

What could I have done to him? What was I capable of?

"What did I do to him?" I ask her, sorry for something I have zero memory of. But like Rhys said, I may not remember what I did, but it doesn't erase what was done.

"You saved his life. And mine. You just had to hurt us to do it," she whispers, a trembling smile on her face.

Her smile tells me so much more than her words do. What I did to her must have been unspeakable.

"I don't remember hurting you, and I don't know what kind of person I was before all of this, but I am sorry you and your husband were hurt. I am sorry for whatever part I had to play in your pain. And I am grateful for your kindness and your protection. I hope to repay it someday."

I didn't think I could feel more alone than I did when I noticed Kyle gone.

I was wrong.

I help Aurelia clean up the glass from the plate, and head back up to my room, swearing to myself I would never be another burden on these good people.

It takes me a long time to realize a few things. One, I never did get to eat. Two, she never accepted my apology. And three, Kyle didn't come back.

17

KYLE—BEFORE

It took weeks to find Iva and Devereux again. They must have felt me closing in on them in New Orleans because I'd never had so many problems searching for someone before. They had to have Witch help, and it pissed me off. Even keeping track of the local and national news did nothing to help. You would think missing children would be plastered on every screen and shouted from every rooftop. Unfortunately, that wasn't the case—the stories were either suppressed by a spell or by the human's own indifference.

I kept my ear to the ground, listening for distressed locals and anything at all about kids. It seemed that was what they were after. Ethereal children with a little extra something to them. Ones maybe Iva would need to fight against one day—at least that was my guess. I was in an upstate New York farm town when I heard of a large group of kids missing, and I knew I had to move faster.

I wasn't fast enough, and for that I will always carry that stain on my soul.

In the end, I couldn't find her—I had to find him, and he was much easier to locate. All I had to do was search for someone without a soul. In today's society, you'd be surprised how low the number actually is.

By the time I followed them to Maine and the dilapidated but stately mansion on a clifftop overlooking the north Atlantic, they had claimed another victim—several more victims. Tiny mounds of freshly hewn graves dotted the floor of the forest butting up against the property, the mark of souls tainted the air and the innocence of them tore at me. The horror of it all brought me to my knees, bile forcing its way up my throat.

I could feel the dead. I could feel the savage cries of children that hung on the whipping wind and I could take no more.

Not one more child would die at my inaction.

Not a single one.

It didn't matter that killing Nicola's body would

surely kill my heart and stain my soul. Both were already dead from the things I'd seen and felt. The only thing that mattered was stopping this death.

My heart didn't matter at all.

I left the clifftop and traveled to private elevator for the penthouse apartment that housed my King and Queen. And they were mine. I refused to acknowledge the Witch part of me. I refused to pay homage to a species of people who would help do this. Someone was hiding Iva. Someone was covering the deaths up. Someone warded the Emerson's house. Someone brought Devereux back. Someone helped bring Iva back from Hell.

That someone had to be a Witch. There was no other way to hide from me, no other way to suppress this much death. Tessa was gone, but there had to be someone else. She couldn't have worked alone.

My feet touched down on the marble tile inside the closed elevator, and I raised a finger to the stylized 'P' for the penthouse. As the lift carried me up, I forced myself to meet my own dead eyes in the mirrored wall.

I deserved this guilt. I earned it. I waited too long. I should have come here sooner.

But just couldn't bring myself to do it.

When the elevator dinged its arrival at the top floor,

I was met with Aidan's blade to my throat as soon as the doors opened.

"Ky?" Aidan asked, startled. I didn't exactly blame him. I hadn't checked in at all since the day I was fit enough to stand on my own two feet.

"Get West. We have a problem," was all I could bring myself to say. I could have gone with an apology or at least asked how he was dealing with the upheaval of his whole freaking life, but I was too focused on my task to be a decent friend.

"Yeah, man, follow me," he replied, no questions asked and I followed him down the hall to a wide bedroom door where he pounded for a good five minutes. The door was finally ripped open by a pissed off West.

"Are you fucking kidding me?" West whispered to Aidan as he opened the door. It takes him a second to realize Aidan isn't alone, but I guess that is my fault for showing up at three o'clock in the morning.

"Jesus, man," he muttered while giving me a quick slap on the back in greeting. "What happened?" he asked getting right to it.

"We need to wake Evan. I'm not saying this shit twice," my voice came out gruffer than I wanted, but the message was the same. I couldn't say it twice. I couldn't order the death of my woman's body and possibly her soul more than once.

Just the once might kill me.

I turned from them and walked woodenly toward the living area, trying not to lose it.

Soon, the room filled with people, the buzz of talking voices grating on my nerves. They didn't know. How could they? It wasn't their world crumbling to nothing.

"Alright, out with it. What are we dealing with here?" Evangeline ordered, and I couldn't contain my flinch.

"I-I found her," I began, "She and that guy Devereux have been hopping from one place to another. Hopping all over the goddamn planet. St-stealing children from families, teenagers, preschoolers, b-babies... I tried. I tried to get them back. To follow them to keep the children alive. But I lost her so many times, and I... She's holed up in some abandoned mansion in the wilds of Maine or some shit. Th-there are graves..."

I stopped then. How could I tell them the scene in Tennessee was nothing? That I'd seen the aftermath when they were moving too fast or were too careless to dispose of the bodies?

"When you... when you stop her, can you make sure it doesn't hurt? Can you... It isn't her fault. It's the dirty fucking soul they stuck in her. It isn't her. Just don't... Don't make it hurt, okay?" I pleaded searching Evangeline's face for sympathy, for mercy, for anything that would tell me Nicola wouldn't suffer.

"Yes. I can make it painless," West said, his gruff voice breaking our stare-down.

If it were him, I could've trusted it, but it couldn't be him to kill her. Nicola told me so herself. If I'd known what she meant I would have left her then. I would have gone far and wide to keep from getting caught. I would have done anything she asked so they wouldn't have used me against her.

I was the only reason she was in this mess in the first place. If it weren't for me, she could have held out longer. I failed her. I didn't listen, and I would regret it until the day I died.

"It can't be you. Nic told me before this happened. She said that the only way for Iva to be killed was if Evangeline did it. It was one of the last things she told me before I was captured. And I-I want your word you'll... you'll..." I couldn't make the words pass my lips. If I spoke them out loud it would be all too real.

Evan came over to me and wraps her tiny arms around my shoulders.

"I know this is hard, Ky. I could see how much you loved Nicola, but she's gone. I'm so sorry, but she's gone," she whispers in my ear, and I couldn't stop the tears from leaking out of me.

"I just have one question. Are you bound?" she asked, and I shook my head.

"She wouldn't let me. Never said why, but I figure she knew this might happen," I croaked.

"We'll be humane about it, but it needs to happen. Iva won't stop, and if she hasn't already, she's about to start a war," Evangeline said carefully, looking me right in the eye.

"I'll tell you where they are, but you'll have to get in on your own. I can't help you kill her," I admitted not saying what I truly meant.

I couldn't help them kill her because I'd likely already be dead. I was going to see my Nicola one last time before it was all over.

KYLE—AFTER

It didn't matter that it was late October in the Rocky Mountains, I was still sweating my ass off climbing this fucking path. As soon I left Mena's front porch I knew I had to get my head on straight.

The memories of everything that we'd been through, the battle, the last time I saw Nicola before Evan worked her mojo and got Iva out of her...

The walls were closing in on me, and I couldn't stay there and pretend I wasn't losing my mind. Nic deserved better than what she got. She deserved better than the shitty life she lead, better than me. It makes me almost wish I hadn't bound her—almost.

I made it to the summit of a substantial trail, still cursing myself that I decided to actually fucking hike this motherfucker of a mountain. Kyle plus thin mountain air plus zero desire to ever do cardio equals one tired bastard.

Maybe it was the lack of oxygen or just me getting over my own shit, but I still had hope. I just needed to get the memory of what was out of my head. Those two weeks might not come back to her. She might not remember the violin I got her or our first kiss or any of the million and one things we talked about in those two weeks, but we had forever to make new memories.

When she first woke up, I wasn't sure it was her. Her eyes were different and she didn't remember me or us. But then so many things that were singular to Nicola alone surfaced and I knew it didn't matter if she could remember us or not.

I did and that was all I needed.

It was full night by the time I made it down the trail and back to Asher and Mena's. Yeah, I could have traveled, but getting my head on straight evidently meant physical exertion.

The house is dark save for the porch light and one lone lamp in the living room. I bypass the locked door and travel directly to my Shortcake. I find her sleeping, curled into a tiny ball, huddled under the covers, the dried tracks of tears staining her temples.

I feel like a first-rate asshole.

I'll make it up to you, Shortcake. That's a fucking promise.

18

NICOLA—AFTER

THE FEATHER-LIGHT TOUCH OF LIPS AGAINST MY TEMPLE filters through the heavy fog of crying-jag-induced exhaustion. The lips trail to each of my eyes, kissing the lids, and I can't help but open them to find Kyle sitting on the bed in the crook of my legs. His face is close to mine, each hand planted in the bed, so his whole big body surrounds me.

"I'm sorry I left you, Shortcake," he murmurs, and his voice is so gentle and so much of what I need, I can't hold the tears back. I want to be mad at him for leaving me here, but I don't think it crossed his mind how much these people would hate me or how much guilt I would feel for things I couldn't remember.

"Shh, baby. I won't leave you again, I swear," his low voice promises as he scoops me up in his huge arms, sitting me on his lap. His wide hands brush the snarl of curls away from my face, his thumbs catching the tears as they fall and wiping them from my skin.

"It isn't that, Kyle. It's just... I must have done horrible things to these people to have them hate me, and I can't remember."

I don't realize my error until I grasp the look on his face. I've seen his gentle face, the one with the quirked smile and subtle creases at the corners of his eyes. I've seen his pissed off face, the one with fire in his gaze and the hard line of his mouth. I've seen his bald terror face, the one with wide eyes and fear stamped on every inch of him. I barely saw that one before I passed out on the side of the road, but I remember it.

I had not, however, seen his enraged face. This expression is about twelve steps up from the pissed off one. His eyes burn hot before the black bleeds from his pupil out, overtaking the iris, and staining the sclera coal-black.

"They were mean to you? Who was it?" he asks, his voice a menacing growl.

"It doesn't matter," I rush to brush my words aside, praying that he doesn't make it a bigger deal of it than it already is.

"Damn fucking straight it does. Who. The fuck. Was it? I leave my woman in their fucking care, and I come back to her huddled in a damn ball in the bed, tear tracks on her fucking face, exhausted. I left you with your people. I left you with family. It may not have been close family, but I expected you to be welcomed and cared for. If you weren't, it's as much on me as it is on them. Now, who the fuck put tears in your eyes?" he orders.

I have two options. One, I tell him about the Rhys and the 'plate of a thousand pieces' incident. About being left alone for hours in a house I don't know, with people I don't know. About how I have the distinct impression there were a bunch of people here who were avoiding me altogether. But I honestly think I'm being a huge baby about it. Or I could shut his mouth for him and do the one thing I've been dying to do for the last three days.

I pick door number two.

I cross the scant six inches between our faces and press my lips to his. I didn't expect his mouth to be as soft as it is, or for the rough rasp of his beard against my cheek to make me so restless, but they are. Kyle's mouth is only inactive for a single second before he is kissing me back.

Holy shit.

He was my husband. I knew he had to have at least kissed me before. How could my brain forget this? Forget him? How could I forget his scent of outside air, citrus, and man? The way his soft lips harden slightly as they capture mine? And when his tongue touches my lip, asking for permission before it invades my mouth, I can't help but melt against him and let him in. I should probably kick my own ass for forgetting him, but I'll do that later. I was busy.

His arms wind around me, one hand tangled in my mass of hair and one around my waist, and he's holding me so tight, I finally feel warm for the first time all day since he left. My hands find their way to his face, his beard so much softer than I expected it to be against my palms. Kyle's hands move to my hips, lifting me, adjusting me somehow so I'm straddling him, and I can't help the way my hips buck on their own against the thick ridge in his jeans.

Oh. *Oh, shit.*

The groan that comes from him hits me everywhere, and soon, I'm pulling at his shirt, yanking it off of him so my fingers can reach all of his golden skin. Somehow my shirt seems to rest at my waist and the heat of him against the bare skin of my breasts, against the now sensitive points of my nipples makes everything in me clench. I didn't know this is what I wanted, but I'm for damn sure taking it.

I direct my lips to his neck, nibbling the strip of sensitive skin just below his beard line. Fates, what is it about that line that drives me insane. If I had fangs, I'd sink them in right there just so I could taste him. My blunt teeth will just have to do because if I go another second without knowing what his skin tastes like I will lose my mind. As my teeth and tongue make contact, a feral growl rumbles from his chest and I squirm at the vibration of it.

I want.

I didn't think I could, didn't know my body required his touch, but now that I have it, I can't get enough. I want more. Twin points of sharpness meet my neck and the press of it drives me into a frenzy.

I ache.

He moves us and presses me into the mattress, his large body between my legs and the weight of him against me is everything. He moves, rasping his beard over my tender flesh, kissing down my neck to my breasts, pulling my nipples into his mouth and sucking them to ridged peaks. He nibbles at the underside of them and a flash of heat scorches its way through me.

I need.

His wide, rough hands run down my body, taking

the thin camisole, my pajama pants, and underwear with them, and then I'm naked. I should feel cold or awkward, but I don't. I only feel the scorching heat of his gaze on my skin and his rough palms running back up my legs, gently spreading them so he can fit his big body in the space they just vacated as he kneels at the edge of the bed.

Kyle roughly tugs me closer and the power of him, the presence of his stark need, makes me squirm with want. Soft lips and the silky rough of his beard scratches against my skin as he kisses the hollow where my hip and thigh meet and then the wet heat of his tongue licks closer and closer to where I want him.

Tremors of anticipation hit me and he has to hold my hips still just so I don't vibrate myself off of the bed.

"How am I supposed to eat this sweet pussy if you won't sit still? Hmm?" he asks as his tongue takes a quick lick of my center, earning him a strangled moan.

"If you quit your squirming, I promise I'll make it so good for you, Shortcake," he rumbles, his low gravelly voice hitting me hard. My moan in response earns me another, longer, lick. My body feels like it is ready to combust. Goose bumps skate across my skin, but I feel like I am on fire. I feel restless and unembarrassed and nearly mindless, and he has barely even touched me.

"Just as sweet as I remembered," he murmurs

against me and then he fulfills his promise to the letter. The rasp of his beard between my legs, kissing, licking, sucking my clit in between his mouth, devouring me until I can't recognize the sounds coming from my mouth or control what my body is doing.

My hands find their way into his hair, and I am pulling him closer and closer to me, grasping for something I can't name but need more than my next breath.

Pleasepleasepleaseplease.

"Oh, I'm going to give you what you want, Shortcake, but it's good you asked so nicely," he rumbles.

Then, his thick, blunted fingers spear into me and I am lost but I refuse to care because it feels just so fucking good.

"Ky!" I call out as I come, losing myself and my mind in the pleasure of it. I feel obliterated—completely wrecked but I don't want it to end. I want more. I want what's inside those jeans. I want the promise of that bulge. I want all of it.

Kyle grabs his discarded shirt and wipes his mouth and beard with it, cleaning up the mess I made all over his face. Why does that naughty thought just rile me up again?

When he tugs the top button of his jeans free, I'm

back to squirming, but I don't stay that way. I move. Sitting up, I take over and rip his jeans open, and reaching in to take my prize.

Holy. Shit.

I underestimated what I was getting. I won the fucking cock lottery with Kyle. I can't measure exactly, but it doesn't really matter. This thing is going to split me in two and I'm going to love every single second of it.

Suddenly, I feel like we are moving too slowly. I want him on top of me, in me, moving with me. I want his sweat on my skin and his mouth on mine. Circling my fingers around him, I give him a single stroke. He gives me a little shudder of want, and I've never felt more powerful.

I did that.

"Fuck, baby," he groans and the feral growl that rips up his throat should make me fearful, but it doesn't. It does the exact opposite, and I reach up to his face and pull him down to my mouth, tasting his lips and my come on his tongue, and the mix of the two just drives my need higher.

One quick lick into his mouth, and I find myself flat on my back again with Kyle climbing up and over me. He fits himself between my legs, notching his cock at my opening and slowly pressing himself into me. I stretch around him, and the ache of it feels so fucking good. It isn't just his cock, it is the groan I pull from him, it's his heat against my body. It is the safety and the pleasure and the pull at my heart. It is the way he stills before planting his elbows in the bed, tangling his hands in my hair and scorching me with a kiss so full of promise, I clench around him—my arms, my pussy, my legs. All of me is pulling him into me wanting to absorb him, love him.

"Are you mine, Shortcake?" he asks me as he runs his lips over my neck, pulling more at my heart that he has to ask. Of course I am. Of course I'm his. I nod to answer, but it isn't what he wants.

"You have to say it. You have to say you're mine. I need to hear the words," he murmurs his plea as his eyes meet mine and he singes his way into my soul.

"I can't remember us and I love you anyway. I'm yours. I'll always be yours," I whisper back, reaching my neck up so my mouth can meet his, our tongues tangling in a delicate dance of promise.

Then we move together, burning each other up, climbing higher and higher. Our kiss breaks and his lips are back at my ear.

"You're mine and I'm yours, Shortcake. Forever," he whispers in my ear. "Say it, Nicola. Tell me."

I want to tell him I'm scared of what's coming. That

I don't know what the future brings and I am so scared of what I can't remember. But I don't. I tell him the truth as I know it because in this moment, I know we can beat whatever comes at us.

His thrusts move faster and faster, our release barreling down on us.

"You're mine, Ky. Forever," I murmur on a moan.

When the twin points of his fangs slice into the place where my neck and shoulder meet, I only feel bliss.

19

KYLE—AFTER

If I were to venture a guess, Nicola only kissed me to shut me up. Other people might have been offended, but I'm not. I've been dying for those pale, rose lips for months.

My eyes latch onto the already healed double crescent scar my fangs left on her shoulder. It is the mark she should have had months ago, and the pride I feel at looking at it should send me into another frenzy of lovemaking, but Nicola is finally sleeping, and I don't want to wake her. Her body needs the rest because I have plans for it for the rest of our lives.

I refuse to sleep, though. I have to find out why my

Shortcake was crying, stowed away up here when she had a whole house-full of family downstairs. Pulling on my discarded jeans and searching for a new shirt, I dress and make my way downstairs. The main floor is empty, but I know there is a training center downstairs in the basement.

Mena and Asher's house is the new hub for the Phoenixes. Mena and Aurelia have been teaching the Oracles to defend themselves in a fight as well as making sure the Soldiers are adequately trained. There was a mountain of messes for them to clean up after Iva was taken down. They let anyone who wanted to leave the Legion go without repercussions. They let the Seers choose their own fate, and they banned all ceremonies that included the forced blinding and eye removal of a Seer.

They are still working out the kinks, and Aurelia has still not chosen a Secondary, but they are making strides. I only know this because I've kept an ear to the ground. Plus, you'd be surprised how many people just flap their gums around me because they assume my silence means I'm not listening.

Oh, I am, cupcake. You better fucking believe it.

I open the steel reinforced door masquerading as oak. It matches all of the other doors in the house, but I know this specialty made door is fire-proof, has a bolt-action seal, and can withstand a battering ram, and probably a pound of C-4. I feel the warding of it. No one can get in if they weren't welcomed into the home first. The spell is delicate in its intricacies, but stronger than the steel reinforcing the oak. Whoever cast it is stronger than even I am, and while I'm not proud of my Witch heritage right now, I have to give credit where it is due. The faint crackle of green at the edges makes me think Max is the source of the magic, and I'm impressed.

Something tells me Max is stronger than I thought. *Good to know.*

The room beyond the magic is buzzing with conversation and activity. Ian and Aidan are sparring with bokkens at the center of the space. If Aidan is here, Evan must be as well, but I don't see her.

I do see West and Cam trading punches in the ring, and Asher and Carver in fencing outfits trading blows with shiny rapiers. I wince internally at the sight of Carver. So much had happened while I was gone that I didn't hear for a long time about Carver's husband, Javier. Javier had been a spy for the Emersons, holed up inside the King and Queen's own house, and his machinations had brought the deaths of John and Olivia even after Aurelia took him out. The bastard.

I peel my eyes from Carver to seek out Rhys. I find him having a discussion with Max and another, taller woman I haven't met yet. The unknown woman is gesturing wildly with her hands. I'm confused at her vehemence until I realize she is signing, and Rhys is translating for her to Max.

I owe my hide to almost every single person here, so it sucks that I have to bite the hand that fed me, but fucking hell. It is high time I settle some shit and air out the dirty laundry of familial fucking drama.

If I had to bet money, Rhys—and not Aurelia—is the one I'd have to talk to anyway. I remember how he reacted to her months ago before all of this shit started. If I hadn't gotten in between them, who knows what he would have done.

I travel the scant twenty yards, getting right in Rhys' space. Out of the corner of my eye, I see Max yank the woman out of the way. Towering over him, I let Rhys know just how pissed off I am by the low warning growl that rumbles through my chest.

"I want to know why I found my wife upstairs, alone, crying herself to sleep when I left her with family. Care to explain that to me?" I spit.

Rhys' face morphs from surprised to pissed in an instant.

"Wife? What the fuck, man? You bond her while she

was out or what?" He sounds vaguely angry, but I don't have the time or inclination to deal with this topic again. I said my piece already and the story hasn't changed.

"I explained that shit to your wife already. I don't have to explain it to you. And that doesn't answer my fucking question. Why. Was. Nic. Crying?" My growl says I mean business and his face says he feels fucking guilty.

Jackpot on the first try.

"Why are you asking me? I'm not the only one in this house, you know," he evades.

"Oh, I don't know. Deductive fucking reasoning? Of all the people who I've seen interact with her, you've been the only one who has been overtly hostile. I ventured a fucking guess," I deadpan waiting for him to deny it.

"Fine. It was probably me, but you have no idea what Nicola did to us. You have no idea what kind of pain she caused," he counters, defensive.

"Says who? You think I didn't ask her after I watched you try and strike a blind woman? What are you, high? You think I don't know exactly what she did and why she did it? You think that wasn't my first fucking question?" I yell, pissed.

"And she just told you. When has Nicola Miller ever

been forthcoming with information?" he asks, and even though I can see his point, on this issue, he is in the wrong.

"Maybe when she thought she was going to die? Or when she knew she could trust me? Or when she knew I was her mate? Dealer's fucking choice, Rhys."

"So out with it, then. Tell me. Why did Nicola do this to us? Why did she put us through this? I can't get a fucking paper cut without hurting my wife, Kyle. Who would be that cruel?"

I hate that I have to do this. I wish Nic could remember all of the moves she had to make to keep Rhys and the rest of her family alive.

"It wasn't cruelty. It was the only way you and Aurelia would live. Every path she saw had her dying at Iva's hands, but when she tied her life to yours, she had to be careful, she had to stay out of certain battles that would have gotten her killed. It got her to run and hide, and it got you to protect her when you would have given up. Nicola used to be able to see a lot more than just death, Rhys. She used to be able to see so much more. And you can think Nic's an evil bitch all you want to, but she kept you and Aurelia alive. She kept Mena alive even when every single move she made was being watched, and every path she took could have killed you all and herself. You have no fucking clue. Nicola has been abandoned, used, hung out to dry, hated, and vilified all to keep her family alive. And you ungrateful little shit, can't even wrap your head around the fact that she may have done it for a fucking reason."

Rhys' expression is a mix of guilt, devastation, and rage, but his lips stay closed.

"Do you have any idea what she has gone through to keep you breathing? Who do you think nudged your brother into telling you his plan for Olivia when he was supposed to keep it a secret? Do you know how many steps she took just to get Evangeline born? To make sure Iva was destroyed? She sacrificed her body and her soul to make sure I lived. You and I both have no idea how many people she has saved along the way or how many she saved before they were ever born by taking out Iva. So if you can't be a decent fucking person to her, I need to know. Because I'm making sure she doesn't get treated like shit for the rest of her whole goddamn life. That's a fucking promise," I challenge.

A hand clamps down on my shoulder, and I look back to find the hand is attached to West. Aurelia, Mena, and Evangeline are right behind him. Mena is silently crying and semi-shoves West out of the way to wrap her arms around my middle.

"Thank you. I've been trying to tell them, but they didn't get it. Thanks for getting it," she murmurs before giving me a quick squeeze and letting me go.

The woman I don't know shoves two fingers into Rhys' chest and then starts signing, her chocolate brown eyes blazing fire. Furiously moving her hands and mouthing the words that don't seem to pass her lips. I can't read her lips, but I don't want to be on the receiving end of their ire.

"Samara, honey, stop. I get it. I'll do my best to stop being an asshole," Rhys replies to her flurry of movement, but isn't signing back. Either she can hear or her lip reading skills are unparalleled.

Samara gives him a scalding look and huffs as she turns from him to leave the room.

"What did she say?" Max asks.

"She said that Nicola saved her life, and if I didn't quit being an asshole she would figure out how to lift Aurelia's and my bond just so she could snap my neck," Rhys mutters as he rubs a hand down his face.

I can't stop the full belly laugh the bursts from me which starts a chain reaction because Ian is rolling on the ground holding his stomach laughing, Aidan is gasping for breath as he laughs himself sick, and even Rhys, who looks embarrassed as hell, is chuckling.

"Okay, I was an asshole. I'll tell her I'm sorry and try

to avoid my dickhead ways in the future. We good?" he asks me.

"We're good, but if you make her cry again, I'm making you bleed and that's a fucking promise," I warn him.

"Duly noted."

20

NICOLA—AFTER

I STRODE TOWARD A DILAPIDATED WHITE MANSION, MY SHOES kicking up tiny puffs of dust on the dirt drive. The Spanish moss hung from every single tree on the property as well as the wide portico. A blonde man waited for me there, leaning against one of the thick columns, calm as you please.

His presence annoyed me, but I masked my irritation with a smile. He was so much easier to manipulate if he thought he was making me happy. Like I could be happy with a child. That was all Devereux Emerson was. He was less than that. He was a soulless tool I could wield at my leisure. If he fell, there were plenty more right behind him to do my bidding.

He really was only good for one thing, but even that was

lackluster. I guess it was my fault for picking a soulless minion. When the coming battle was won, I would replace him with a newer model. Maybe someone with a little more heft to him.

Maybe Kyle would do, but I would have to work him over first. He was a bit too shiny, a bit too good for my taste.

"I have the perfect one for you, Mistress," Devereux crooned, and I fought rolling my eyes. Yes, he needed replacing post haste.

"Good. Show me your offering. It had better not be like the sad specimen you found me in the Quarter. I'll not take another charlatan, Devereux."

"But Mistress..."

"I'll not take another one of your excuses, either. Now, show me what you have," I ordered, flicking my fingers to get him to move.

The last one was a child of a so-called Voodoo Queen. The Voodoo Queen herself had been a two-bit hack from New Jersey with a fake Cajun accent. Her child, however, had been the product of a drunken Mardi Gras night with a Warlock, and her teenage son had been powerful—but not nearly enough.

None of them had been thus far. None of them were what I needed—none have been able to sustain me for anything longer than a month.

Devereux led me to the tattered remnants of a once

opulent sitting room. Flood waters had ruined most of the mansion but were especially unkind to this room. The hardwoods were bowed, the ceiling crumbling in some places, missing altogether in others, and the patterned wallpaper was falling off the walls. Honestly, could he not find a better place for this? It reeked of mildew and swamp and fear leaking from the child sitting bound in the middle of the room.

Sigils written in bone dust marked the circle around her, holding her stationary until I could arrive. How thoughtful. The girl could be no more than four, and by her scent, she was a wolf. If Devereux had to tether her to that spot with sigils, then she must be powerful. We would see how much.

She was such a little thing, tethering should be unnecessary. I was beginning to doubt his skills at scouting. It wasn't until I touched her did my faith in him come back. He had done well with this one.

Everything about the girl's past and future flashed through me. The girl's name was Mya. If her path had not crossed mine, she would have been an alpha, a pack leader— one of the first female alphas in three centuries. She would lead an uprising against the members of the Ethereal who oppressed the wolves, and she would bear children just as powerful as she. Her line would grow and prosper, and the wolves would be equals with the other shifters.

Such potential in such a little body. Yes. This would

sustain me for more than a month. Maybe three. Her body stayed immobile while I looked her over. White-blonde hair, green eyes, and a dainty upturned nose. She would have been a beautiful girl and done important things.

Pity.

Devereux's voice started chanting then. A well-oiled machine of convenience, he was. Maybe I wouldn't get rid of him just yet. It would be so difficult to train a new one. It wasn't as easy to control the minds of others now that my power source had been stripped.

All those Aegis ashes gone to waste...

Devereux's voice broke through my musings, and I recognized the point in the spell where I would need to play my part.

"Vivifica me morti et artis. Det vobis spiritum meum, quod nutrit animam," I murmured the words as I watched her chest bow from the crumbling floor and the life drain from her eyes.

She still breathed, but her soul was mine now. The unease in my stomach that I was so good at hiding lessened some and I wasn't quite as hungry as I had been. Success.

"Do what you will with the girl, but I will need another before the week is up. Don't fail me, Devereux, or I'll have you replaced. Understand?"

I didn't really need a soul so soon, but better he have one

ready than have him with me and have to endure his incessant pawing and fawning. I'd rather keep him busy.

"Y-yes, Mistress," Devereux's said, the frown on his face a sweet little pucker. I did so enjoy ruining his fun.

I removed myself from the dank-smelling room, turning from him, and heading back to the road and the waiting town car sitting on the street instead of the drive. I couldn't have the poor lad driving me scared out of his brain if he heard the chanting and spells. New Orleans or not, humans rarely liked it when they witnessed the Ethereal.

As my shoes hit the dirt drive once again, I picked up the faint scream of the girl as Devereux took his fill. Revenants were always doing nasty business, but good help is hard to come by.

The young chap saw me coming and hustled to open my door for me, his mocha skin paling slightly when a last gurgling scream from the girl rent through the air.

"W-what was that?" he asked.

"No idea. Maybe an animal of some sort?" I offered, sliding into the leather seat.

"Yeah. You're right," the driver murmured, but I heard the disbelief in his tone as he tugged at the collar of his chauffeur uniform.

Oh, bother. I was going to have to dispose of this driver, too. Well, only after he got me to where I was going.

"Where to, Miss?" he asked once he'd shut my door and settled himself into the driver's seat.

"The airport will do, thank you."

My eyes flash open to a nearly pitch-black room, the only light coming from the open blinds and the faint shine of moonlight filtering through the pane. Sweat slicks my skin, and my hands won't stop shaking as they yank the covers away from my naked legs. Despite the sweat, I feel chilled to the bone. That wasn't a vision, it was a memory. From before I woke up in Knoxville. It had to be. There wasn't another way to explain it. It wasn't a dream—it felt too real. And that child...

Mya. Her name was Mya.

Oh, God. I stole her soul. I left her to that man. Oh, God. She's dead—I know it—and it's my fault.

Gorge rises in my throat, and I bolt to the bathroom, emptying the meager contents of my stomach into the toilet. My hands clutch the cold porcelain, and I try to block them out but the thoughts that come refuse to be denied.

Mya was a wolf. She was why the wolves wanted

me. Why they came for me. They didn't want Kyle. They wanted me. I was right before. It was my fault.

Did he know? Did Kyle know what I'd done? Did the rest of them?

They couldn't know. No one would harbor someone like me. No one good, anyway, and Kyle was good. I knew it deep in my soul that the man I loved wasn't evil or wrong. There was no way he knew what I really was.

My mind snags on something I said. *I will need another before the week is up.*

Oh, God. Oh, no. Nononononononononono…

How many? How many children did I kill? How many souls did I steal? The tears that come do nothing to wash away the stain on my soul. I am tainted, worse than garbage. I am evil—or at least I was.

Kyle didn't deserve someone like me. He didn't deserve someone who stole life—there was no redeeming my actions. None.

My brain screams at me, hurling insults I don't want to accept. *Killer. Murderer. Thief. Murderer. Murderer. Murderer!*

I shouldn't have woken up in that hospital. I shouldn't be breathing. Not after that. Not after what I've done.

I don't deserve to live.

Steeling my spine, I pick myself up off the floor,

wash out my mouth, and go to the dresser where my clothes have been meticulously organized, butting right next to his. I pull one of his shirts from the stack and breath it in before putting it back on top. I dress in the warmest clothes I can find and leave the rest. I won't need them where I'm going.

I find a paper and pen on top of the dresser and write a quick note, leaving it on the bed. Then I pull on a pair of thick socks and pick up my boots, so no one will hear me when I leave the house. With my hand on the door, I look back to the white square of paper resting on his pillow.

I wish I wouldn't have woken up. I wish I wouldn't have given myself over to Kyle or kissed him or hugged him. I wish my taint weren't all over his skin. He deserved better.

I hope he finds it when I'm gone.

21

KYLE—AFTER

BY THE TIME RHYS AND I IRONED OUT OUR SHIT AND HAD A light sparring session, I'd been gone from Nicola for at least two hours, if not more. Staying down here wasn't a choice I made lightly, but if I thought she was doing anything but sleeping, I would've been upstairs in a heartbeat. I hated being away from her, so I made my excuses and headed for the door. I missed her skin and her sleepy smile, and I needed to taste her lips a few million more times before I would be sated.

I was just glad they didn't hate her. Of all the people I would expect to actually loathe Nicola, Aurelia was one of her more vocal supporters. She had first-hand experience of Iva digging around in her brain and sympathized more than anyone. It was good so many were on her side. We'd need their help down the line if the wolf shit started heating up.

As soon as I cross Max's ward, a heavy pit forms in my stomach. All I feel is agony –in my gut, my heart, my head. My gut clenches and my heart feels ripped in two. Something is wrong.

I don't wait to travel from the basement hallway to our room. But she isn't there. I flip on the lights and check the bathroom. Fuck I even check under the damn bed and the closet, but it's empty. My gut is telling me she isn't even in a fifty-mile radius of this house and when my eye catches on a white slip of paper on my pillow I fight the urge to rip this whole fucking house apart.

With trembling fingers, I reach for the paper, not wanting it to be what I already know it is.

> KYLE,
> YOU DESERVE SO MUCH BETTER THAN TO BE LOVED BY SOMEONE LIKE ME. I'VE GONE TO RIGHT MY WRONGS. DON'T LOOK FOR ME. I'M GOING WHERE YOU CANNOT FOLLOW.
> NICOLA

It takes five full minutes for her words to sink in and

when they do, my fist closes around the paper, crushing it into a little ball. I tuck it away in my pocket before I lose it completely. In a rage, I rip the lamp from the bedside table and throw it across the room. The bed is next, and the mattress gets flipped into the next wall. The dresser meets my wrath, as well as the walls and curtains. But the chair gets the worst of it when I rip the plush fabric and upholstery in half with my bare hands. A roar breaks from my chest as I fling the pieces hard enough to embed the wooden frame into the wall.

She left. She fucking left me.

KYLE—BEFORE

I didn't put much thought into coming here. All I knew was I had to say goodbye before there was nothing left to her. A part of me envied humans. When their loved ones died, there was a monument to them—there were remains. There was something tangible on this earth to hold onto. When a member of the Ethereal died, all we had were ashes—fragile things that could be blown away by a stiff breeze.

I had to say goodbye before there was no more to her—that was my only thought. I didn't think about my safety or Evangeline's plan of attack or the outcome.

For once, I was selfish. It was what I needed. Not

anyone else. I was probably fucking things up, but I didn't really care. I needed this before I died.

My boots crunched in the pine needles as I walked from the tree line toward the two-story, coastal Maine house. I knew I wasn't alone in these woods, but it didn't matter.

None of it did.

When my first boot made contact with the porch steps, the front door whipped open. Standing in the doorway was my Shortcake.

Or what was left of her.

The hair was the same, the curls fanned away from her face in a fiery red mane. Her body was the same, but everything else was different. Her beautiful blue eyes had muddied to amber. The set of her shoulders and the cock to her hip. That wasn't her. That wasn't my Nicola.

Seeing it again killed me—it felt worse than walking through that forest of dead children, worse than watching Devereux's hands on her skin. Worse than losing her the first time. Because I was only getting to say goodbye to her shell. I wouldn't hear her laugh or listen to her hilarious British curses or watch her play the violin. I wouldn't get to kiss her or tell her goodbye.

Nicola—the woman I loved more than my own soul —was gone.

Iva was talking to me, saying something about how

she knew I would come, but I ignored her words and thought my final goodbyes.

The first blow seemed to come from nowhere. One second I was on the porch, staring at the body of the woman I loved, and the next punches and kicks rained down on me. I didn't realize at first that they were coming from her or just how strong Iva was. It made sense. With each new soul, she got stronger, with each life she took, she absorbed a little more power.

I didn't fight back. Not when she picked me up by my shirtfront and threw me across the room, or when she drug me by my hair back to the starting point and started all over again.

I should have protected her better, I should have made sure I listened to her when she tried to warn me. Iva was standing there because I failed Nicola, and I accepted my beating for that reason alone.

I felt my lips split and bones break, felt my skin bruise and all the while I never made an attempt to fight back. I didn't come here for that. But for every second I didn't strike back, Iva lost her cool. Her rage climbed higher and higher.

"What? Did Nicola take your balls when she took your heart, Kyle?" she taunted as she circled me, the heels of her shoes clicking on the hardwood floor.

She didn't realize she was giving me what I wanted, so I kept my mouth shut and gave her a bloody smile.

KYLE—AFTER

I sink to my knees, my eyes scanning the destruction of the room, my brain silent. I can't think. Why would she leave—that is the real question. She had a reason—*I've gone to right my wrongs.*

Where would she go?

I need a direction, Shortcake. Please just give me that.

"Kyle?" Evangeline's voice filters in from the doorway behind me. "Wh-what happened? Where is Nicola?"

"She's gone," I murmur.

What I don't say is I'll find her. And I have an idea where she's gone. As my gut tells me to head southeast, my idea gains wings. I know where she went.

I'm headed to New Orleans.

22

NICOLA—AFTER

STEALING A CAR WAS EASIER THAN I THOUGHT IT WOULD BE. Getting the hang of driving it, however, is a challenge. I found the shiny car keys on the entryway table of Mena's home and snagged them as I walked out of the door. I wasn't sure what part of my brain was running this show, but some autonomous part of me was supplying information.

Put on your boots once you're outside. It will be quieter. See that shiny emblem with the horse on it? Pick those up.

Pressing the tiny unlock button, lights flashed in the driveway. Even in the darkness, the car shone, but the front end was illuminated by the porch lights, and I decided the color was somewhere between red and wine with a flat black double stripe down the center of the hood, roof and back end. It looks mean and beautiful, and I can't help but recognize the color. Max's car was the exact same one. If I were going to ride out to my death, I picked a good car to do it in. I did a quick circle around it, a single finger brushing over the word 'Mustang' before dropping into the driver seat and figuring out the ignition.

Kyle said I was one hundred percent blind before, so it was doubtful I'd ever driven. Even in that single memory, I'd had a driver. But I could see in that memory. It didn't make any sense...

It didn't matter if it made sense or not. I know what I did—there wasn't an excuse or reason I could accept. I had to do this.

A part of me—the part that was selfish and needy— wanted to stop. She wanted to stay here with Kyle. She wanted to forget what she saw in that memory or at least tell Kyle first. She wanted to know if he would still love her. I knew he would not, and even if he did, I didn't deserve to be loved by him. I didn't deserve his warm smile or the rasp from his beard on my cheek when he kissed me.

I didn't earn that kind of love.

My eyes snag on a bright red ignition button, but when I press it, it does nothing. *Press the brake with your foot, then press it again*, the other part of me supplies. The engine roars to life, and I let that part of me that knows where she is going and what to do lead the way. That part of me adjusts the seat and mirrors, throws the car into drive and rockets her way south, leaving me to trail behind her wallowing in my own self-pity.

I hit a speed bump once I cross the New Mexico border. One, I didn't have any money and the gas gauge was reading less than half a tank. Two, it felt like an icepick was digging a significant hole in my brain. I needed to pull off the road before my brain melted and I wrecked the car. And three, I had the distinct impression I was about to have a vision. The part of my brain that knew more than I did told me I would have a tougher time driving it when I was blinded by a vision.

I see an exit coming up boasting lodging so I take it even though I probably won't find money for a motel room anywhere in the car. If all else fails, I can at least park somewhere before I can't see anymore. The motel advertised on the sign is nothing more than a single story row of rooms with a flickering sign and an empty parking lot. I feel unsafe and conspicuous, like I'm just asking to be robbed and stabbed.

I don't have the luxury of finding a safer spot because as soon as I throw the car into park, a vision hits me like a slap.

AN ELDERLY WOMAN STOOD AT HER KITCHEN WINDOW *washing a sink full of dishes. Beyond the window was her garden and beyond that was a tiny motel.*

The white of her hair stood out against the weathered, paper thin skin of her cheek. Her eyes told of thousands of laughs and smiles. Hundreds of thousands of hugs and kissed boo boos, her gnarled but strong hands spoke of countless cooked meals and full bellies. Arthritis was setting in on her wrists, and she could feel snow coming soon. Fall was edging into winter and her garden's flowers were all but spent. It didn't matter anyway because as she got on in years, there was no one to take care of them. It was hard to cultivate the delicate flowers in the desert landscape, but she did her best.

Her family's motel on the other hand, was much too tiresome. The sign was broken, the town had fallen to disrepair, and even being just off the main highway, few people ever stayed longer than the few hours it took to rest up before they were on the road again. Even those guests were few and far between.

The woman shrugged and pondered if she should sell. A developer has been through about a week back and she still had his card. Her and her husband could move to Arizona or Florida or maybe they should move to Texas to be closer to their children and grand babies. She would think on this some more and make a decision before the week was out.

The woman finished washing that last pot in the sink, rinsing it and setting it in the drainer before heading to bed. Her husband had already gone to bed complaining of a stomach ache. The glutton ate too much of her chili is what it really was. He was always putting too many onions on it, too. The old man would never learn, but it was one of the many things she loved about him.

She dressed in a long nightgown, unpinned her curls, kissed her husband's sleeping cheek, and settled into bed. She fell asleep with a smile on her face, thinking of a move to see her grand babies, and seeing them grow into their own people.

Her breaths slowed farther and farther, and then they stopped altogether.

She didn't wake up.

OH, THAT JUST SUCKS, IS MY FIRST THOUGHT ONCE I FEEL BACK to myself again. My eyesight hasn't quite returned yet, and I am one hundred percent positive I have blood tears running down my face. I recognize the motel in my vision as the one I'm sitting outside, and I don't know how I feel about that. The icepick in my brain is gone, which is a plus, but now I have a call hitting me square in the chest to go to her—to help her move on.

This plan is less than ideal. I'm ill equipped, not knowing exactly how I'm supposed to send her anywhere let alone on to be reborn, not to mention I only have so much time before Kyle will get my note. I don't know exactly how he found Max and me outside of Knoxville, but I'm willing to bet his Tracker vocation has something to do with it.

Still, the pull of her soul yanks on my limbs, and I climb from the low-slung seat. Skirting the main building, my low-heeled boots crunch through the underbrush as I walk carefully toward the little white house at the back of the property. The pull of the soul guides me around the back to the bedroom window. It is a cute little house with chrysanthemums in the painted window boxes and a wraparound porch, perfect for an elderly couple. I could imagine a grandmother sitting on this porch, grandkids swarming her legs, and for some reason that makes me sadder because I know I won't have that. I won't have children with Kyle. Or grandchildren. I won't get to see him smile or make him laugh. I won't get to do any of that if I continue to do what I'm doing.

I don't want to take her soul. It makes me feel

complicit in her death somehow. Like my presence called her to it rather than it happening naturally. But the soul wants to leave and so do I.

The phase rips through me without thought. Fire skates over my skin as a strange tearing sensation rips at my back.

Oh, this hurts. This hurts!

My hands fly to my mouth, muffling the scream that bubbles up from my throat. I hear a distinct rip, and a huge weight hangs from my back.

I have wings. I have fucking wings!

Craning my neck, I try to get a glimpse of them—brilliant orange feathers with dusky black tips. They are so pretty.

I snap back to myself and my purpose here. It isn't to look at my pretty feathers. It is to help a soul. I'm not exactly sure how I am supposed to do it, but I will give it my best shot. The woman I saw was a good woman, and she deserved her rest.

I move closer to the window, trying not to touch the wood of the house, so I don't set it on fire. A piece of me —some intrinsic part of me starts speaking in a language I don't know.

"Libertatem concede tibi ita regenerationis ultra valeamus," I whisper into the blackness of the desert night.

But I know the words. I know what they mean. *I grant you the freedom of rebirth so one day we may meet again.*

It is a prayer. A... funeral rite and a part of me knows it better than I know my own name. This is my purpose, and as I watch trails of light stream from the woman's chest I feel at peace. Her body is still, and her husband will wake up to a loss, but her soul is at peace.

It is then I decide I can't continue on this path. I can't go without talking to Kyle. I did a shitty thing by leaving him. Again. He may not deserve me, but he at least deserves to know why I left, and my vague note probably told him less than nothing.

My fire dies as quickly as it came, the uncomfortable and altogether unpleasant feeling of my wings going back to wherever the hell they came from washes through me, but I make my way back to the car.

My shirt is toast, I feel a little queasy from hunger, but I know I need to go back. I'll talk to Kyle. We'll work it out. Maybe he could explain what happened. Was I spelled into killing that girl? It didn't feel like myself. It felt vile and dark and evil, and I couldn't just throw myself literally to the wolves for something I didn't understand.

Kyle would explain what happened and we would go from there. Nodding, I reach for the door to the car feeling less like I was walking into a death sentence and more like I was making progress.

I hear a shuffle of feet drawing my eyes up to the empty parking lot. Chills skate down my spine and I scan the lot to see what made that sound. When a ball of red sails over the roof of the car and hits me square in the chest, I'm surprised.

Shit, I think as I fall to my back on the dirty asphalt, and my light goes out.

23

KYLE—AFTER

I flinch when Evangeline's hand touches me. I left her to trail after me as I made my way back down here from the room I tore to pieces upstairs. I've been stuffing weapons from the training room into a duffle bag for the last five minutes and ignoring her completely for the last ten. I have a plan—sort of—and I know where I'm going... Maybe. This is the shit I have been worried about since the first time I was able to wheel my ass into her room. Fucking repercussions. Fucking Iva.

Fuck, fuck, motherfucking fuck!

Hadn't we been through enough? I had two weeks with her before everything fell apart. Two weeks before I endured over a month of torture. Then, I had five and a half months of searching for her fucking puppeteer, four months plus a few weeks of her in a coma, and one single night with her back in my arms before I lost her all over again. Seriously? Could we catch a goddamn break already?

It isn't until Evan pinches me on the underside of my arm do I quit overstuffing the duffle.

"What?" I growl, pissed off I have to stop what I'm doing. Hell, I'm pissed off anyway, but this just sprinkles a little bit of extra lighter fluid on top of an already blazing inferno.

"Where are you going, what are you doing, and if you talk to me like that again, I'm going to have your balls as a fucking necklace. Remember who you are talking to, Kyle."

If she weren't a woman, my Queen, and a friend...

"Pardon me, my liege. I have to go stop my wife before she gets herself killed, oh and fun fact, get me killed as well. She's headed southeast—toward the wolves. You know, the wolves that just tried to kill her? I'm sorry if I can't give you more information than that, but it seems my wife was a little lackadaisical with the fucking details. I've got my bond, a shitty ass goodbye note to work with here and fuck all else," I rant turning back to my weapons.

Nicola must have remembered something. I didn't

know how I knew she was going to New Orleans, I just did. Sure there were a fuckton of factions in between there and here, but a lot of them didn't make sense. The wolves did.

"You have family here. People who can kinda see the future, a Wraith or two and a Witch with an attitude—total compliment BTW—it isn't like you need to go off to war alone, big man," she replies, ignoring my attitude altogether.

"Where were they? Huh? How did she get out of the house? How did she make it so far away from me that I only have a fucking direction and a sense of dread? Goddamn it!" I roar, tossing the weapons bag onto the floor of the training center.

Max and that damn ward. She's too powerful. She didn't just ward for threats—that working held back bond ties, visions, everything. No one is supposed to be that fucking strong. And she was able to take it down without a single problem.

Wards are complicated magic—they take massive amounts of power to bring up and take down, and she just snapped her fingers and boom. No ward. What the fucking fuck?

"I'm sorry, okay!" Max pipes in from across the room. "I had to make it strong to keep Wraiths from being able to travel in. How was I supposed to know it was going to turn into a magical fucking dead zone?"

"Maybe if you learned from an elder or consulted with another Witch instead of figuring shit out as you go, you wouldn't fuck something like this up!"

"Well, it isn't like you practice anymore, so it looks like I'm shit out of luck," she fires back before taking a deep breath and pinching the bridge of her nose. "Look, I know you're pissed, but attacking me isn't going to help."

She's right. I haven't practiced since I realized Iva had Witch help. I didn't want to associate with that part of myself. I could be helping Max develop her abilities—from what I gathered, she had been ostracized from her family and had no one to turn to about stuff like this. My comment was dickish in the extreme. Plus, I should have noticed the ward was wrong as soon as I crossed it. It was as much my fault as hers for making it.

"You're right. I'm sorry I was a dick," I apologize, feeling like an asshole. I remember not having a coven to go to for help. It sucks.

"Yeah, well, you've got a reason. If you didn't I would have handed Evan the knife to cut off your balls," she shrugs.

"She took my fucking car!" Ian thunders from the

door, his voice booming through the training center like a bomb.

"Your wife took my Mustang, Kyle. Do you know how long it has been since I've gotten a new car? Nineteen eighty motherfucking five, Kyle, and she took my brand fucking new Mustang. I've driven that woman around more times than I could count when she was blind. I know her ass doesn't know how to drive. I swear to everything holy, if there is one goddamn scratch on it, I am taking it out of your hide!"

Max stifles a snicker, and his eyes cut to her, scorching fire.

"It's not funny, *Maxima*," he zings, knowing Max goes by her nickname for a reason. At the utterance of her given name, her face sobers.

"Don't taunt me, *niñito*. I'm older, stronger, and I can snap my fingers and turn your infantile ass to dust," Max threatens, the tip of her finger sparking green magic as she points to him in her ire.

It's funny as hell, but I don't have time to deal with this shit or the obvious shit storm that is brewing between these two. I just hope Nic and I are far, far away when these two explode.

If you can get to her before she does something stupid, you mean, a snotty little voice inside my head snarks.

"Look, this is amusing and all, but I have bigger problems than whatever sexual tension you two are working with. Now, I'm leaving. If you're coming, come the fuck on. I'm running out of time."

I reach down and grab the duffle but stop short when West forms right between me and the door.

"Sorry, brother, but there is no way I'm letting you do this alone. The last time you went off on your own, you damn near got yourself killed."

"Got you killed, you mean," I mumble.

"No. I don't. That battle was coming long before you tossed your hat in, man. I don't blame you for one bit of it. I don't blame Nicola either. The both of you have gotten a raw deal. I just want to make sure everyone comes home safe," West explains, his hands raised in a placating gesture.

"Whatever, man. But we have to go now-ish. If you're coming, let's go. Nic's in pain, and I don't have the time to wait for you."

"Do you know where you're going?" Aurelia asks from behind West. When she and Rhys came in the room, I have no idea.

"Southeast. I'm thinking NOLA, and my gut says wolves. I can't explain why. It's just the worst kill I saw was a wolf girl. It was the most brutal—the most savage. I can see repercussions from that one coming faster than the others. Plus, we already had a wolf problem. It just makes sense to me."

She takes a moment to ponder my answer, but I don't have time for this.

"I'm hopping to her instead of driving, so if you want to come, find someone who can travel and let's go."

"I'm in," Mena says grabbing Asher's hand. "But you're staying here," she orders, pointing to Aurelia and Rhys.

"What?" Aurelia screeches.

"Chain of command, pumpkin pie. Both of us can't be in the shit, and you have babies. You can take the next one, though. Deal?"

"This is bullshit. But fine," Aurelia grumbles.

"We're in," Evan murmurs, which means West, Cam, and Aidan are in too.

"You'll probably need a medic and a sniper, but someone needs to give me a lift," Ian says exasperatedly.

"Aww. Come on, bro. You know you want to hit something. What's more fun than shifter fights?" Aidan cajoles.

Shifter fights? What. The. Fuck? Sometimes the brothers scare the shit out of me.

Ian just gives his brother a baleful glance.

"Shifter fights? I'm in. Those fuckers made me

demolish my baby. I rebuilt her from the frame out, and now I have to start all over again, the fuckers. Who brings the cars into it? That's just mean," Max throws her hat in.

"I'm staying. Nothing against you and your lady, Ky, but the last time these two were left unsupervised, they gave us all a heart attack," Carver explains as he gestures to Aurelia and Rhys.

"Fine. Let's go, and stay close," I order.

Traveling without a set destination in mind is hard, and in a group this size, damn near impossible. But hopping from one location to another with a direction in mind makes it easier. Well, it's faster than driving, at least. I keep close to Interstate 25, traveling twenty miles at a time, stopping to feel Nicola's direction and starting all over again. Our only break was to stop to let Max puke, so she didn't soil Cam with her dinner.

We got close to the Colorado-New Mexico border before I couldn't go any farther. Nicola's heart rate sped and then... *nothing.*

I felt nothing. Not her emotions, not her heart in my chest, not her presence. Nothing.

"Fuck! I lost her!" I roar, my feet crunching in the rocks and desert brush in the mountain pass close to the border.

"What do mean you lost her?" West asks, bewildered.

"There's nothing. I can't feel her. What does that mean?" I ask, panic setting in. This hasn't happened to him. He's never lost Evangeline even before they bonded.

"I don't know," West whispers his reply.

"I'm going to New Orleans. Now," I murmur before smoking out from the mountain pass and arriving at the outskirts of the city.

If I can't find her, I'm going to someone who will.

Or else.

24

KYLE—AFTER

THE LOT OF US ARRIVE IN ONE OF THE SEVERAL SWAMPLAND wildlife refuges around Lake Pontchartrain, well outside the New Orleans city limits. This refuge is located on an inlet between Lake Pontchartrain and Lake Borgne, and the land seems to dwindle beneath our feet as marshland encroaches on the solid ground. How people live here, I don't know, but I wouldn't hate on their lifestyle. It wasn't my place to judge.

What I would hate on was their desire for my wife's head.

We walk at a sedate pace into what appears to be a packed campground. I knew it wasn't what it looks to be in the least. This wasn't transitory residences or people on a camping vacation. This was a pack.

In my scouting of Iva's practices, I came across one of several dens of wolves in and around New Orleans. Some had been hastily abandoned—the stench of death lingering in the soil where unlucky ones met their ends —but this one regularly had occupants. Some wolves lived in secret in the Quarter—hell, all over the country —but the majority of surviving wolves lived in packs either here near the swamps or in the Appalachians far away from the majority of the population.

Tents, campers, and a few RV's were positioned in a wide circle around a rather large bonfire. Some were pup tents, some were newer, ten-man Coleman ones. The RV's were old—at least a decade or two past new— but they seemed to be kept-up and in good repair. Several people—men, women, children—surrounded the fire on log benches. They were talking, joking, shooting the shit. No one was keeping watch, no security. This told me more about these people than anything. They didn't fear the outside world or they didn't expect people to actually come here. The land might be protected somehow, but it didn't keep us out, so I doubted it.

This wasn't exactly my best plan, but I knew who I needed to talk to and I knew I had enough backup to level the whole damn state if need be. With the amount of families, I didn't want to start anything that would get innocent people killed or hurt. I smelled no evil here, all I smelled was wolf.

Just as we are about to breach the circle, I'm elbowed out of the way by Max. I try to yank her back, but she snaps her fingers and my fingertips burn when I touch her. Shit. Max is a wildcard in every single sense of the word.

"Excuse me!" Max yells getting everyone's attention.

The yelling wasn't necessary. Max commands attention with the blue hair pinned up in what I'm gathering is her signature victory rolls, the tattoos which cover nearly all of her available skin, the Rockabilly clothes, and the obvious signature of power written all over her. A wave of tension hits me, and I feel the hairs on my arms stand on end. She got their attention all right.

"Hi everybody! My name is Max, and I have a grievance to share with your Alpha. May I speak with him, please?" she says sweetly. I've known her for approximately three seconds and even I know her sweet voice is not a good thing.

A stout man with dark hair, graying at his temples rises from his spot on one of the logs surrounding the fire, meeting us at the break between a twenty-year-old RV and a derelict camper. His eyes are an odd bottle green, and they flick to each of us, studying each person before settling back on Max.

"Hello, Max. My name is Scott. I'm the leader here. How can I help you?" His voice is soft and his manner is polite. Although he senses the aggression coming from us and the double scoop of crazy coming from Max, he doesn't engage. Interesting.

"A pair of wolves used my fully restored Chevelle as a bumper car. I would like to know why," Max says calmly.

Scott's mouth quirks for a moment as he crosses his arms.

"Was this incident just outside of Knoxville?" he asks, his voice full of mirth.

"Got it in one," she replies, crossing her arms to match him.

"Well, Max, those wolves weren't a part of our pack. They were cast out about a year ago for deciding to become a Witch's lapdog doing mercenary tasks for money. We don't allow that sort around here," Scott says stonily.

"Fascinating. If they were cast out, who gave them orders? And why was a pack surrounding the hospital, Scott?" Max counters.

"Those two are among the Nameless. We don't speak of the ones we cast out. We sure as hell don't give them orders. Especially since you and I both know those two boys are dead as a doornail. What I want to know is where is Nicola? Why isn't she with you?"

"How do you know Nicola?" Max asks just as I break in with, "You don't have her?"

"Where is my wife, Scott? She was headed here before I lost her. I know someone took her. I want to know where my fucking wife is. Now," I growl, the phase overtaking me before I can blink. My fangs break free, elongating my jaw. My talons erupt from my fingers.

My phase triggers a chain reaction. The men, women and children who were so benignly sitting around the campfire are not so benign now. Men and women jump to their wolf forms, children scurry away, toddlers and babies carried away by older children. Snarls and snaps of teeth reverberate through the open space.

"I don't mean anyone any harm unless they've hurt her. I just. Want. My. Wife," I growl, trying to calm my voice and avoid an all-out brawl.

"No one here would have hurt Nicola Miller. We owe her our lives. She's kept Iva from exterminating our pack altogether."

Do they not know? I don't want to be the one to tell them but if they don't know I'd rather explain now.

"But... Iva killed a wolf child. She..." I trail off.

"Was wearing Nicola's skin?" Scott finishes my sentence. "Yeah. We know. The benefit of being a wolf is we can smell the difference. We know it wasn't her. Hell, we even moved in to protect her in Knoxville before we realized ya'll were friendlies."

"That pack was you guys? You were there to help her?" Evangeline throws in.

"Yeah, we got there a little late. You two slipped out while one of our younger pups was keeping watch. He didn't recognize you and said you did something to disguise her face. It didn't help ya'll were downwind," Scott explains.

"Whoops. My bad," Max murmurs earning a guttural growl from me.

"So if you don't have Nicola and you wanted to protect her, who the fuck has her?" I mutter to myself.

"I hate to point this out, but I'd venture a guess that Witches have her, don't they?" Cam asks from behind me, and we all—myself included—turn to look at the usually antagonistic man.

"You said the men who attacked Max and Nicola were Witch's lapdogs. You said they were mercenaries. They were probably under Witch orders. Witches were the ones to kick you guys out of the hospital. Witches helped Iva. Witches attacked Aurelia and Rhys. Duh, guys. I'm not that smart and I put it together," Cam says shrugging.

But if Witches have her, how do we get her back?

"Do you want me to try and locate her? I'm pretty sure I can't fuck that up," Max offers shrugging sheepishly.

The horrible part of all this is, Max hasn't really done anything wrong. She disguised her so the wolves couldn't discern her identity. She did exactly what she was supposed to do. How was she supposed to know they were friendlies? And some of them weren't friendly at all.

"Fine. If you can find her where the bond cannot, by all means, go ahead."

"Gimme a second and I can try to get a bead on her. Do you have anything of hers?"

"No, but I'm bonded to her. I'm hers. Will that be enough?" I reply.

"Maybe," she murmurs as she grabs my hand, closes her eyes and begins murmuring in Latin. Her words are ones I've uttered more times than I can count. *"Inveniam quod quaero. Ostende mihi,"* she murmurs on loop, the grip of her hand cutting off the blood supply to my own.

Find me what I seek. Reveal it to me.

When Max's eyes open again I know she has the same result I did when I searched our bond over and over again.

Nothing.

25

NICOLA—AFTER

I FEEL MY BODY LONG BEFORE I CAN ACTUALLY OPEN MY EYES. As it were, my body is slung over a shoulder, blood is rushing to my head, and for as little as I know, I am damn certain I have a concussion. This is proved when my body is slung off of the shoulder and onto the hard ground because I cannot hold in the moan of pain as the landing jars my whole body.

Clutching my head, I desperately try not to vomit as I hear a woman chuckling in the background. When a boot plants itself into my ribs with enough force to knock me into a wall, my moan turns into a scream. I'm pretty sure I heard a rib snap.

"Wakey, wakey!" a shrill woman's voice calls.

Bitch, I'm already awake, I think as I force my heavy lids open. What the hell did I get hit with? A spell?

My eyes try to focus, but either the spell still is affecting me or the concussion is. When I can finally see one room instead of two, I try to inspect my surroundings. The motel room is less than five-star, more like a shabby shithole. A double bed sits right across from me with a tattered bright orange coverlet. The carpet smells like old shoes, mildew and dirt with a side of magic—which to me is reminiscent of ozone and melted pennies—thrown in. The walls are a dirty taupe color are littered with scratches, dents, and other unidentifiable stains.

A blonde woman kneels down to study me. She is beautiful in an odd, off-putting sort of way. Her features are too sharp, her cheekbones could cut glass, and although her eyes are a stunning ice blue, they have a coldness to them that scares the shit out of me.

"Oh, goodie. You're awake," she deadpans as she grabs the front of my ripped sweater and yanks me up from the floor, passing me off to someone else.

It is only then that I realize she has a man with her, and I can tell by his build he's probably the one who kicked me in the ribs. He's blonde, his eyes and features match the woman's as well. They have to be related. The man is only a slightly smaller build than Kyle.

Oh, God. Kyle.

My thoughts turn to my husband. Why did I leave him? Why did I do that without talking to him? Why was I so stupid?

"Put her in a chair and tie her up," the woman orders, the bored tone of her voice sending chills through me.

"What do you want? What did I ever do to you?" I ask on a whisper, struggling against the hands holding me. A quick whisper and my struggles die, my body falling like a rag doll in his arms.

"Gag her while you're at it, will you, Baron?" she mutters as she turns from us to stare at a timeworn book. It is thick with a leather binding and yellowed pages. He whispers again, and it is like a switch has been flipped, and my voice has been turned off.

The man, Baron, wraps my wrists with thin but chafing ropes, tying me tightly to a wooden armchair. He pulls my boots and socks off and lifts my pant legs, wrapping the rope around the skin of my ankles. Methodically making sure when I can move again, I won't want to.

Making sure if I struggle, I will bleed.

"Now, you've never done a single thing to me. But your family? They've hurt mine. Aurelia Constantine in particular, burned our mother alive. I'd consider cutting her directly, but I don't need Aurelia. I do, however, need you. You are going to help me."

Aurelia burned someone alive? That seems... extreme.

I wonder what her mother did to make Aurelia do that. She doesn't seem to be someone who kills without thought. And what the hell can I possibly help this crazy woman with? I'm betting whatever it is, I don't want to do it.

"I see by the confusion on your face, you have no idea what you really are. You aren't just a Phoenix; you aren't just an Oracle. You're a piece of the Veil. You stand on both sides of life and death. Death calls to you. Death can be molded by you, and souls can be resurrected through you. And that part of it is useful to me." I'm going to bring my mother back, Nicola. And you're going to help."

What the hell is she talking about? A part of me wonders if she's crazy, while the other part knows she is but also knows she isn't lying.

"My name is Bella, by the way. You and I are going to become great friends," she says, and another flash of red hits me in the chest.

Lights out. Again.

NICOLA—CUTLER, MAINE 2016

It was dark here, stuffed inside this hole inside my subconscious. I knew what I was getting into when I said yes, knew the consequences of my actions. I knew Iva would be wearing my flesh. What I didn't know was how strong she was. How easily I could be moulded into the little hole I found myself in, how easily I could be gagged and tossed aside, rotting away inside my own head.

Iva's had her fun for months. Killing people with my hands, stealing souls of children, letting that filthy, soulless monster touch my skin. I haven't been awake for all of it, but some of it...

It would be a blessing to forget.

I think she enjoys my pain, my revulsion. It is a feather in her cap to finally bring me down. The insurgent she couldn't find—the one she least expected —not after I bonded Rhys to Aurelia, anyway. She never knew all the things I did to thwart her, and hiding in this little hole inside my brain, she won't. She won't find the people I've hidden away or the steps I took to bring us here.

She won't find out until it is too late.

When Kyle comes calling, though, I almost lose my hold on this one piece of refuge. She relished beating him, but when she realized he wouldn't fight back, wouldn't hit my face or body even though it wasn't me running it, she became enraged.

Iva beat him with my fists, broke bones with them, drew blood with them. And all the while he never once defended himself.

She threw him away, tossing him back to the few people who could help him—who could help me. West was kind enough to reach out a hand and help him up. Kyle barely made it to his feet and struggled to even take a breath.

"Please, Nic. Please make it back to us. Please," Kyle rasped.

"And why would she do that when I am here now? Nicola Miller was a poor blind girl who never did anything but try and scheme her way around me. Now that I'm here, there is no need for her to wonder. She is powerless. There is only me now," she said with my mouth, and I wished at that moment I could kill her. That I could help in some way to bring her down.

I could. I could fight back. I could scream and writhe and break free. I'd kept in the hole to keep my secrets—

to keep the secrets of so many who couldn't help themselves.

But the cavalry was here now. I didn't need to stay hidden. I didn't need to stay quiet in this little slice of hell. I feel Iva's smile droop on my face.

That's right, bitch. You'll be getting it from all sides, now.

I screamed, I writhed. I scratched at the walls of my mind, but it wasn't until Kyle took the blade meant for Evangeline did I feel the first crack in my prison.

Seeing his blood run, seeing the knife in his belly, changed something in this prison. It let the light in, untethered the bonds around my wrists and ankles.

It let me out, and the scream that ripped from my lungs was, for once, my own. They wanted Kyle to go to a hospital. I did too, but I needed to say goodbye to him first.

I wasn't coming back from this, but he could. He would.

"Get him to a fucking hospital!" Evangeline screamed rushing to intercept me as I tried to get to Kyle. She slashed with her rapier, gouging my skin with the razor sharp blade, but it doesn't stop me. It won't stop me from going to him.

"No! No, don't keep me back from him. Please! Kyle!

Please!" I begged, and the look on her face changed from steely determination to unfettered sorrow.

"I'll let you take her soul. I'll hold her back, just please let me say goodbye to him," I pleaded, my eyes flooded with desperate tears, and she let me go.

I scrambled past her, making it to his side faster than I could blink.

Blink... Seeing his face with these new eyes, I realized how beautiful he was, how strong. It didn't matter that his left eye was swollen nearly shut or his lips were split. It didn't matter a single bit because he was mine and I would get this one moment to say goodbye to him. I grabbed his bloodstained cheeks and whispered in his ear.

"I love you. I will always love you. In the next life, in the one after that, on and on until forever. Don't you forget it," I ordered him.

Ian desperately tries to staunch the flow of blood pouring from Kyle's stomach, and I realize I'm hurting him by keeping him here. I moved to let him go, but Kyle's eyes drifted open, and grabs my wrists, holding me to the spot.

"Lo-love you, Nic. See you on the other side," Kyle murmured before his eyes rolled back in his head, and he lost consciousness.

"Noooooooo!" I howl, but Aidan snatched him from me in a swath of black smoke.

Then, I lost my hold on the walls of my prison, and the gates crashed back down on me, stomping me back into my hole.

NICOLA—AFTER

I feel like I've been thrown off a cliff, rolled in acid and then stabbed with the business end of a hot poker. Holy shit, whatever knock-out juice Bella is packing, I want no part of it.

My eyes stay closed partly because if I open them, I may puke, and also to try and assess my situation. By the scent, I'm still in the shitty motel, but something tells me there is another person in the room.

I'm proved right when Bella and another woman begin to argue. I'm only half listening as I mentally check my body. I'm still tied to the chair, but whatever spell Baron hit me with has been lifted.

"I told you and your idiot brothers to fetch her for me. Did you deliver? No. I told you and your idiot brothers not to hurt her. Did you obey me? No. And then you ran off to save your own hide, and you expect payment? No," Bella scolds, her tone scathing.

"I told you what happened. I told you exactly where she would be after I tracked her back to Colorado and followed her down here. I can't control what my brothers did, and the morons got themselves killed. I didn't wreck her car and stab her in the stomach. I stayed on the periphery and assessed the situation while Idiot One and Two made other plans. There was no way I could capture her by myself, so I called you. She still got captured. I deserve at the very least half of the bounty."

This pings in my mind. In my vision, there were three wolves.

Not two.

Three.

She was the third. She was the other wolf. The one who had her maw in Kyle's gut. The bitch.

My eyes flash open, and I assess the two women arguing over payment. I recognize Bella's platinum blonde hair and pale skin, but the other woman I don't know at all. Plus, she's not exactly a woman. She can't be more than fifteen at a push—messy brown hair pulled into a haphazard bun, dirty black skinny jeans, sneakers, and a wearing an odd assortment of shirts. Her white thermal is layered under an open green flannel shirt, under a gray hoodie, all under a denim jacket. How many layers does this girl need? And then her accent registers. She's from the New Orleans pack.

"I would say she deserves at least two-thirds," I mutter and both their eyes swing to me. "I mean, come on. She did spy on me like a fucking creeper and had I not changed my course, her maw would have been in my husband's belly. That's what you meant to do, isn't it? You weren't going to let us go or bring us here. You planned on killing us," I accuse my eyes meeting the gray eyes of the girl's. "So you should give her two-thirds, at least. Give her enough money to run."

26

KYLE—AFTER

THE PACK HAS LEFT US TO OUR OWN DEVICES, GOING BACK TO their bonfire, leaving us newcomers to our problems, but there are still too many people in my space. Too many people comforting me when all the avenues to find Nicola haven't been exhausted. I know they haven't. Even if some of them are things I swore I'd never do again.

"We'll find her," Mena insists as she turns to Asher so he can call Aurelia. Mena still hasn't managed to get around her aversion to electronics—or shall I say, they haven't gotten over their aversion to her. Ash steps away to make the call, and I meet West's eyes. His expression tells me he thinks the worst.

But she can't be dead. I would be too. That is the way the bond works. Right?

"Stop looking at me like that. She's not dead," I growl. I want to get in his face. Fuck, I want to punch him or anything else that will relieve this gnawing ache of fear.

"I don't think she's dead, Ky. I think whatever mojo has the bond blocked might keep Aurelia from finding her. It might keep us all from finding her," he murmurs consolingly.

Might keep me from finding her, he means. But fuck that. Fuck his consolation, fuck his doubt.

"So that means I'm just supposed to give up now? How many years did you follow Evan? How many years did Rhys follow Aurelia? What makes you think I am any different than you? I'll find Nicola. Even if I have to rip this world apart to do it. You got me?" I growl, and if my eyes turn black or my talons grow, well I really don't fucking care.

At this point, I don't give a shit if he's my friend. I don't care if he's my King. No one is keeping me from Nicola.

No one.

But I'm going to have to do the one thing I promised myself I wouldn't do. I'll have to cast a spell. I swore I wouldn't use my magic after the Witches dishonored me—after they broke my ward, bombarded my house and took me from my Nicola. I swore I would never use that part of myself again, but to find Nicola, I would break any promise, deny any oath.

Even to myself.

"Max, we'll have to try together. I'll have to do the working with you. Together... we might be able to reach her," I concede.

Max gives me an appraising look. I think she understands why I have been avoiding that half of myself, why I would choose to deny the part of me that resembles so many dead, so many lost to darkness, so many who have turned into monsters. Finally, she nods.

"Okay," Max murmurs.

"If I add my juice to it, will it help or hurt you? I can't send souls on with a ward working, so I don't know if it will fuck you guys up," Mena offers as she makes it back to our loose circle.

"It can't hurt. If it doesn't work, we'll try it without you," Max answers.

When Mena slips her hand in one of mine and Max the other, the sheer power from both of these women hits me like a sledgehammer.

"*Inveniam quod quaero. Ostende mihi,*" Max begins and I follow, murmuring the words over and over again until they cease to make sense. Nothing happens until

Mena grabs for Max's hand, completing the circuit of power between the three of us. It feels as if a barrier has been lifted. Whatever working they had over Nicola has crumbled to dust. With more acuity than ever before, I have found her.

I can see her in my mind's eye. I can feel her. Her heart beats once again in my chest, her breaths fill my lungs, and the torn, jagged piece of my soul where she had been torn out is healed. I feel almost whole again.

Nicola's tied to a chair in a shitty no-tell motel room. There is dried blood crusted around her nose, but her face is fierce with unspent retribution. I want to rip apart whoever made her bleed. I want to tear them apart with my bare hands.

"I know where she is. I can find her," I murmur, my voice clogged with relief and tinged with rage.

"Where we headed?" Evan pipes in.

"New Mexico."

I'm coming, Shortcake. Sit tight.

Faster than I thought possible, we make it to the outskirts of a property in Raton, New Mexico, a mere twenty miles from where I lost her.

But we have an enormous fucking problem. Sure we know where Nicola is, but getting to her is going to be an issue. Scanning the motel's property, I see about thirty witches in the biggest Witch's circle I have ever seen.

Their focus?

The room where my wife is.

NICOLA—AFTER

Bella's smile is feral. I can tell my words have pissed her right the fuck off, and I couldn't give two shits. She can think I'm trapped all she wants to, but she forgets this whole place is flammable.

And I'm not.

"It won't matter one way or the other what I give Talia or what she's done to you. You won't be here. You won't have a say. You won't be you," Bella informs me, smiling.

"What the fuck are you on about?" I ask to give myself a little more time. I'm not strong enough to phase yet. Whatever mojo the devil twins cooked up hasn't left me completely.

"Did no one tell you what my mother was executed for?" she sneers. "She helped Devereux put Iva inside you, silly. Iva wore you like a party dress, too. Killing children up and down the coasts and everywhere in between. There's blood under your fingernails, sweetheart," Bella says through gritted teeth.

Talia's head swings to appraise Bella, her face one of outrage as bile rises in my throat and the room begins to spin. Does that mean I didn't kill that wolf and Iva did? Does it even matter that it was her inside me if my hands were the ones that killed her? Questions run on loop inside my brain as I struggle not to vomit or hyperventilate. She wants to put her mother inside me.

She wants me to be a puppet.

Before I can scream, before I can cry, before I can say anything at all, she is murmuring in a language I don't know—Latin if I had a guess. Her words run together as her eyes burn red before they close. Magic coats her hands, staining them with crimson light, but no matter how many times she says the words—nothing happens.

Her red eyes flash open, her words are silenced as she rushes me knocking Talia out of the way. She rips at my already torn clothes, searching my skin.

"Where is it? I'll fucking burn it off. There is a mark or sigil keeping me out. Someone protected you. Where the fuck is it?" she screams in my face as she grabs my chin in a bruising grip. Then, her eyes flick to the space where my shoulder and neck meet. She stares at the spot for a moment before her eyes fly wide, and a howling scream erupts from her mouth, piercing my eardrums, making my head swim.

"No! No, no, no!" she screeches as she grabs the

armrests of my chair and flings it and me along with it across the room.

She is going to kill me. She can't use me, so she's going to kill me.

Fire explodes across my skin, burning my bonds in seconds. Talia and Bella advance on me as I try to scramble out of the remnants of the now burning chair. Talia jumps from her human form, her body flashing from human to mist to the thin, rangy wolf I saw in my vision just a few days ago. But she doesn't do what I expect—which is to rip me to shreds. No, instead she throws her body into Bella knocking her sideways as a blast of red magic shoots from her fingers, missing me by inches.

Bella turns her focus onto Talia, aiming her magic at her instead of me. A wave of red slams into the teenager, slamming the wolf into the wall before she fades back into her human form, coughing and sputtering up blood. Bella raises her hands again to hit Talia while she's down.

I move to intervene, but I'm so focused on the women in front of me that I've forgotten I haven't seen Baron since I woke up. Well, I forgot until I feel a blade at my throat.

"You're not the only one who is fireproof, darlin'. Now, put out those flames, or I'll slit your pretty little throat," he whispers in my ear.

"Bella! Stop fucking around. We have bigger problems, sister," he orders.

"What?" Bella screeches but turns from the unconscious Talia, the magic dying on her fingertips.

"We're surrounded. The coven came for us, Bell. We've gotta go."

Somehow, I don't think this is good news for me.

27

KYLE—AFTER

As a child, my grandmama took me once to a coven meeting. I was nine at the time—much too young for such a thing—but she wanted me to see my heritage. She wanted me to see that I had a large family of welcoming people who would embrace me.

Grandmama kept me on the periphery of the circle and told me to watch as they worked a healing spell on a pregnant human from the next town. The human knew her baby was sick, and begged the coven to help. She offered payment, anything, but the coven would not take a single coin. The coven would never take money for healing. Not ever.

Grandmama said they were good people, and they

healed the woman as they held hands and danced around in the moonlight. Celebrating life—no matter the species.

There is no dancing here tonight. No healing. This coven does not want to help us or anyone else but themselves. There was a time I believed otherwise.

I shrug off the weapons bag, unzipping it and fishing out what I need. Had I known I would be dealing with Witches, I would have prepared differently. Turning to West, I pass him a short sword and he gives me a look that tells me all I need to know. He heads left as I go right, drifting closer to the circle. Aidan, Evan, and Cam follow him, and Max and Ian follow me—the eight of us moving equidistantly around the green-tinged circle of Witches. I see a place where I can break the working—in between an older and younger woman but as I move to strike, I'm frozen to the spot.

I fight the spell, fight with all I have in me, but all I am able to do is turn my eyes to Max.

"Don't. That's my mother—my family," she orders, her voice hard. I feel the disbelief and betrayal on my face.

Reading me in an instant, she gives me a withering look.

"I didn't know they were here. I froze them, too. I'm seeing what's going on before people get killed. Don't you dare make me feel bad for that," Max replies to my silent censure with gritted teeth.

Max steps carefully close to the circle without crossing it—if she were to cross it in the middle of a working, she could not only kill herself, but everyone else connected to and inside the circle. Smart girl.

"Mama, what are you doing here?" Max asks the older woman. Now that I am really looking at her, I realize I should have recognized the resemblance.

When she doesn't get a response, she rolls her eyes and then taps her mother's forehead with two fingers, more than likely giving her mother the autonomy of her own mouth.

"Maxima Christina Alcado, if you were still in the coven, I would have you sent to the counsel for this. How dare you interrupt a work–" her mother's words break off when Max taps her forehead again—freezing her mouth.

Max turns to the younger woman instead, tapping her forehead to get an answer.

"Talk, Maria," she orders the younger woman.

"Bella and Baron are in there. They want to bring Tessa back. We're stopping them," she says succinctly.

"Bring her back? How?"

"How did they bring Iva back? Nicola is a piece of the veil. They are going to try to use her again. We're.

Stopping. Them," Maria replies snottily as if Max is stupid.

The way Maria says it, I don't think she's talking about fuzzy bunnies and fucking lollipops.

"But... Nicola's in there. A working this size, could kill whoever is in the center of it. Not just Bella, not just Baron. It could kill Nicola, too. Phoenix or no, she might not be able to survive it. What are you doing?" Max argues.

"I did not decide," is all Maria replies with, her eyes downcast.

This tells me all I need to know. They don't plan on saving Nicola. They are stopping Bella and Baron without any regard to my wife's life. They would rather destroy Nicola along with these awful people than figure out a way to get her out safely.

Now, I need to figure out how to break this working without killing anyone, pissing off a coven full of kill-happy witches, or letting Baron and Bella go.

Tall order.

NICOLA—AFTER

Baron still has a knife to my throat when Bella's shrill scream of frustration breaks from her lips. She begins pacing the short thoroughfare between the far wall and the double bed.

"Now, I'm not sure if you remember this, but you and I have met before. You were a bit blinder then, though," Baron whispers in my ear when Bella turns her back to us.

I don't know if this statement is supposed to make me feel at ease with him or has the intended and successful purpose of creeping me the fuck out.

"I don't know you," I say through gritted teeth. Part of me doesn't want to piss him off because he still has a knife to my throat. The other part of me wants to tell him to fuck off.

"Oh, you will," he murmurs and then lowers the knife, skirting around me to join his sister. The knife's blade is an odd orangey-pink color, and looks to be made of some sort of crystal.

Morganite, my brain supplies. Kyle said something about it. What did he say? '*The only thing that can kill you is a Morganite blade or an Aegis.*'

Oh shit.

Bella's pacing back and forth next to the inert Talia, and every time she passes her, Bella looks like she's contemplating kicking the young wolf.

I look behind me, irritated there are no back exits to this stupid room. To my left is a tiny bathroom with a narrow window over the shower inset that seems more for show than an actual exit. I could potentially burn the room down, but I have a few problems with that plan of action. One, Baron seems to be fireproof. I have no idea how or why, but that is an issue. Two, Talia just tried to save my ass. Burning her alive would be a full-scale dick move.

"They won't do a working with all of us in here, right? I mean they wouldn't kill her, would they?" Bella asks her brother as she gnaws on her thumbnail. I assume they are referring to me, but hell, Talia could be important. Maybe.

"Bell, I don't think they give a shit one way or the other as long as our mother doesn't come back. You know the coven. Not that I blame them. Killing children is frowned upon," he says as he sidles me with a sidelong glance.

"Well, I'm not dying in a shitty motel room in the middle of nowhere New Mexico, that's for damn certain," Bella replies and shoots past him, snatching the blade from his fingers as she goes.

"It's time to see how well they like hostage situations," Bella says smiling, the business end of the knife pointing right at my face.

KYLE—AFTER

There are times where you feel as if you have been staying still. Times where the past seems to always bite you in the ass. Times where history repeats itself over and over again. But seeing a knife to Nicola's throat, I finally understand why she would go through anything to save the people she loves.

Because watching someone you love hurt, watching them in danger, is the worst sort of torture. It limits your options down to one thing: sacrifice. I would do anything to trade places with her. When three people emerge from the hotel room, we are all still frozen. The working of the circle has stalled as two women and a man walk out into the parking lot.

Nicola comes out first, and the first thing I notice is how her sweater is ripped, dipping off one shoulder exposing the bonding mark and a fair amount of her pale flesh. The second, is the orangey-pink hue of a Morganite blade against the delicate skin of her neck held by a hand of a woman I can only assume is Bella.

Rage ignites inside of me—a flash fire over my skin and I fight against the hold of Max's freezing spell. Then, I don't have to fight against it anymore because Max has released me. She has released everyone.

Everything seems to go in slow motion. Nicola's face

morphs from surprise at the number of people around her to elation when she spots me. Then swift, steely determination passes over her features and I know what she'll do before she does it.

Nicola's phase washes over her, fire blazing over her skin so fast that no one is prepared for it. Nicola brings her burning hands up and clutches Bella's knife arm, ripping the blade away while Bella screams in agony.

But she's not watching her back and the man is reaching for Bella, reaching for Nicola, heedless of her flames.

"Max! Break the circle!" Mena screams, her phase already upon her. Blue flames licking up her arms and legs, the glint of a katana in her hand.

Max isn't fast enough for Evan's liking because one second the Witches are standing, the working stalled but still in play, and the next, every Witch has flown back ten feet and is firmly planted on their ass.

The working dissolves in an instant, and instead of the man staying and fighting, he grabs the injured Bella and the pair of them disappear in a ball of red light.

I rush to Nicola, her flames dying the second she spots me, and then she is in my arms again.

"Holy shit, Shortcake. Holy shit," I murmur into her hair.

"I'm sorry. I'm so sorry," Nicola sobs. "I shouldn't have left. I should have asked you what happened."

"What..." I begin, but I'm cut off by a woman's scream.

"What have you done?" Max's mother screeches. "You let them get away! They'll just try this again until they bring her back! Goddammit!"

"But... Bella couldn't work the spell. She was going to but she said something was blocking her. And she freaked out when she saw this mark on my shoulder," Nicola replies as she points to her bonding mark.

Max's mother stops short eyeing the crescent scar with surprise.

"The bonding mark?" she asks incredulously. "You're telling me that little scar kept her from using your powers?"

"It isn't that much of a stretch," Mena supplies from behind her. Mena's phase is still upon her and it takes me less than a second to realize she thinks the threat is still upon us.

"The bonding mark ties two people body and soul, Teresa. She cannot be used in this way again, so the threat of Tessa is gone. It's time for you to go," Evangeline orders from beside Mena.

West appears behind us, Aidan and Cam at his side. Asher, Ian and Max of all people moving in front of us, creating a circle of their own around Nicola and I. They are protecting us from the Witches, making sure we're safe.

"You would choose them over us, Maxima? How can you be so cold?" Teresa asks her daughter.

Max's hard exterior cracks for a moment as the hurt slips past her guard, but she manages to bring the wall back up before she speaks again.

"You kicked me out of the coven because I was too strong, mama. You made me live a lonely, abandoned existence with no family whatsoever. Why wouldn't I choose people who have cared for me and sheltered me? It's more than you've done," Max replies.

The rage on Teresa's face heralds the green magic sparking on her fingertips.

"Teresa, this is not a war you want," Mena warns, "We are on your side when it comes to bringing Tessa back. We do not want that either, but if you do what my sister says you are contemplating, I will make sure you and anyone who thinks the execution of an innocent woman is just fucking dandy face the full retribution of both the Phoenix faction and the Wraith." Mena's words strike a chord with Teresa because her magic dies and she takes a full step back from us closer to her coven.

"Nicola is blood, a part of both factions. So, the

question you need to ask yourself is: do you value your life? Do you value your coven's life?" Evangeline snarls. "We don't want war. But hurting Nicola will start one. Do you understand me?"

Teresa nods, saying nothing to Evan as she calls for her sisters to depart—the lot of them huddling together before disappearing in in a huge ball of green light.

That's not disconcerting or anything.

"Now that the danger is over, where the fuck is my car?" Ian's voice breaks through the fog of lingering adrenaline and I can't help but chuckle.

"Grand theft auto, Shortcake? I like your style," I murmur in Nicola's ear.

"I aim to please."

EPILOGUE

NICOLA—AFTER

"This is where we started, Shortcake," Kyle murmurs in my ear as we touch down on the soft bed of pine needles outside a gorgeous gray-green cabin with a cherry stained wrap around porch.

The metal roof gleams in spots where the sun filters through the trees. The cold almost-winter wind whips through the trees, and for the first time in weeks, I feel like I can breathe.

A week after our brush with the coven, Mena and Evan were sent a missive from Teresa stating in no uncertain terms should Kyle or I ever go looking for Baron or Bella. As far as I knew, the Witch situation was tense at best, and with Max on 'our' side, best was solidly in our rearview.

Bella and Baron were the last people I wanted to find. No offense to the Witches, but I was lucky to escape from them with my head still attached.

How dumb could I be? I choose life, thank you very much.

In the aftermath, we did find Ian's car. It didn't have a scratch on it, but he was still pissed I took it. He softened only marginally when I gave him a hug and a kiss on the cheek, but I didn't foresee any joyrides in my future.

Kyle and I went back to the motel to look for Talia. I wanted to thank her—to get her some medical attention or at least get her a shower and a good meal. But when we went back to the room to help her, she was long gone.

We tried to stay at Mena and Asher's house, but with everyone there and the tension under that roof from the Witch threat looming over us, Kyle felt it was better for us to break out on our own. I agreed, feeling that I drew way too much bad stuff my way with everything that had happened. We did wait to leave until after he told me a heavily redacted version of what Iva did in my body. I felt violated and half insane and the tensions of brewing unrest only made it worse.

Kyle took me away from there and brought me here to his house in the heavily wooded foothills of the Appalachians. We walk hand in hand toward a single story, ranch-style cabin.

As soon as a single toe touches the first wooden porch step, I'm hit with what I can only assume is a memory.

"You're not all Wraith, are you?" I murmured to myself.

"Nope," he answered as he moved away from me, opened the fridge, grabbed a bottle and popped the top.

A wall descended at his blunt answer. It wasn't a slight. Only a marvel. I had always hated the 'stay within your own kind' rhetoric.

We were just people. We loved who we loved.

"So loquacious. Sore subject?" I asked.

"It isn't something I talk about. My mother was a Witch. My father was a Wraith. They were bonded, and she died when I was a boy, taking my father with her when she went. I lived with my grandmama—my mama's mother—until I was old enough to be on my own."

"I bet your grandmother taught you everything there

was to know about spells, didn't she?" I asked, imagining a naughty Kyle casting workings.

"She taught me enough to be dangerous—more to myself than to anyone else," he said as he plunked his beer on the counter. And then he was in my space, swiveling the barstool he so carefully placed me one so he stood between my legs.

"You don't care, do you?" he asked as he cupped my chin in his rough palm.

His question pissed me off.

Why would I care? Because Iva did? Because of my station? He didn't realize I had been slighted my whole life because of my blindness. Put in another category, labeled as 'other' when women in my own faction blinded themselves on purpose.

But I'm other.

Hypocrites.

"Of course not! No one can decide the circumstances of their birth. Blaming someone for their lineage is... is... utter bullshit," I spat, tripping over the audible curse word.

His lips found mine then, and I was lost.

"You kissed me for the first time while I was sitting at a barstool in your kitchen," I murmur, frozen to the spot as I wrap my brain around the fact that I'm remembering my time before—before my body was stolen.

Tears hit my eyes as that memory washes away a bit of the filth that seems to stain me.

"Yeah, Shortcake. Do you want to come inside? You might be able to remember more," Kyle murmurs as he wraps me up in his warm arms.

"Yes. I think I do," I answer him and he sets me back on my feet, grabbing my hand and leading me inside our home.

Thank you so much for reading Shade Kissed. Nicola & Kyle burrowed into my heart and just wouldn't let go. But we aren't quite done yet! Next up is Nicola & Kyle's finale and all the heart wrenching, forbidden mates chaos that is to come.

Sight Kissed is next on the menu, and I hope you're buckled in to see the forgetful, former oracle and her swoony, over-protective mate.

Grab Sight Kissed today!

Want the skinny on future releases without having to follow me absolutely everywhere on social media?

Text "LEGION" to (844) 311-5791

We failed. Now they're coming for us.

My memories are finally returning... And I don't want them. I don't want to know what evil my hands are capable of when the happiness I've found is so close to slipping through my fingers.

But when a friend comes to me for help, I'm once again thrust into a dangerous supernatural war - in a world I still don't know.

And the secrets buried beneath my skin could kill us all.

NICOLA

My brand new eyes flashed open. It had been so long since I had eyes, or a body for that matter. I'd been stuck in the middle—not heaven, not hell—simply a gray formless void where voices called, but I could not come. Where I did enough calling of my own, but only one person heard me.

Only one person came to my aid, because he'd been there in that misty gray place once himself.

I'd repay him, in time, but first I had to gain my bearings. This body was smaller than I was used to. My limbs felt fragile and delicate, but I knew their former owner very well. To say this turn of events made me practically giddy was a vast understatement.

Nicola deserved this. She practically put me here herself with all her double dealings. You'd think the little wretch would count her lucky stars. I plucked her from veritable squalor and all I get for my trouble was machinations and backstabbing.

Served her right.

My new eyes scanned the circular chamber, falling first on the pale blond hair of my rescuer. Devereux Emerson wanted only one thing from me—a deal with the devil, so to speak—and he would pledge his life in exchange for it. What he didn't know was I would have done it for free, but I wouldn't be who I was today if I wasted an opportunity.

"Iva? Is it you?" Devereux murmured reverently while clutching a double-edged Morganite knife in a loose grip. I could understand his caution; this form of Necromancy was forbidden for a reason.

Sometimes you don't exactly get who you asked for.

"It took you long enough," I chided as he helped me to sitting and I glanced around the room. It smelled of fear, blood, and death. Hundreds of men, women, and children had died in this room. I felt their power, and a large part of me thirsted for it—desired the cloying call of a soul that could sustain me.

"I suppose you'll be wanting your payment then?"

He didn't have to say, I already knew exactly what he wanted. The one and only thing Devereux desired was to watch his father die. Walter Emerson earned his son's wrath, and I was all too happy to settle my debt to him in this way.

"If you would be so kind, Mistress. I believe I have done everything asked of me," Devereux murmured as he found his knees.

Bowing already? I could get used to this level of reverence.

"We shall see if you have or have not. Are the children

ready?" I asked. "I'm hungry and if you want your favor, you'll need to feed me."

"Y-yes, Mistress," he stumbled over his words, eager to mete out his justice.

I didn't care either way. I merely needed my meal. My stomach was clawing at me in hunger, and I was too new to this body to go without.

Quick as a hiccup, Devereux came back with a tasty morsel of an eight-year-old girl. She wouldn't be enough.

But she was a start.

Nightmares wouldn't be so bad if they were fake.

If they were just made-up pictures in my head, I could deal with whatever my mind cooked up and move on. But I knew the horrors in my brain really happened, and when you know each nightmare is unearthing layer after layer of an evil that wore my skin like a fucking party dress, well... Sleep is no longer my friend. Sleep is currently my enemy.

And that's saying something.

I've been awake, laying here in the protective circle of Kyle's arms for at least twenty minutes trying to calm my heart down. Every single time I close my eyes, I see what Iva did in my skin. I see the lives she took, and it kills me.

I know if I move a single millimeter, Kyle will wake up and I can't handle the look he'll have on his face. I know exactly what it will be—the exhausted pull of his brow, the fear coiling behind his eyes, the firm press of his lips mashing together so he doesn't say the wrong thing. His voice will be calm and sweet, and it will cut at me worse than the dreams do.

I can't handle sweet when I feel so guilty. My hands did horrible things—my hands, my voice, my body— and dreaming about each life these hands took, makes me want to pull a Lady Macbeth and scrape my own skin off to get them clean. I find it funny that I know who Lady Macbeth is but I can't remember if I have a middle name or not. Like I can't remember all of the things she did in my skin, but I know she did them. And I know my hands won't come clean no matter what I do or how many lives I may have saved along the way.

Not that I can remember saving them.

The past is coming back to me in bits and pieces— never enough to complete the wide-open gaps in my brain or fill in the gaping holes in Kyle's redacted version of events. He tells me the good things. The things I can be proud of. But he never tells me how I hurt people—how I hurt my family—for my own ends.

But I know some of what happened. I know some of the worst sins on my soul weren't committed by Iva while she wore my skin.

They were mine alone.

"I know you're awake, Shortcake," Ky whispers in my ear, the rough tickle of his whiskers brushes the soft skin of my shoulder. "Were you planning on getting any sleep tonight or is sitting there stewing your primary objective?"

"How long have you been awake?" I answer his question with one of my own. I'm not sure if deflection is an innate or learned behavior for me, and at this very second, I hate I don't know this about myself.

I hate I'm deflecting at all.

"When you have a nightmare, darlin', you don't exactly sleep quiet. I was awake before you were," Kyle whispers, but I can hear the exhausted thread of worry in his voice, and it kills me.

We're here, in his violated sanctuary of a cabin—violated because of me, no less—because I can't deal with the guilt piled on my shoulders. It was supposed to be a break, a respite from my Phoenix family, but I'm worse here. I don't see the good things between us like I did when we first got here. I don't see the kisses and banter and touches anymore.

I only see glimpses of what Iva did.

"I'm sorry," I say automatically, gritting my teeth at the words I loathe passing my lips. It has been happening more and more often these days.

"You've got to stop saying sorry, Shortcake," Ky murmurs against my skin as he tightens the band of his arms. "You didn't do anything wrong."

But I did. I did several things wrong.

The self-loathing I'd been shoring up inside me for these last few weeks, bursts like a decrepit dam from my chest.

"I hate it when you say that. You and I both know there is a fuck of a lot to be sorry for," my voice cracks like a whip into the silence.

Suddenly, I lose Kyle's arms when he shoves up from the bed and tosses his legs over the side. Knifing up, he snatches his black boxer briefs and steps into them. His back to me, the tight line of his shoulders catches the light from the full moon filtering through the windows. His hands ball into fists, the knuckles turning white with the strain, and I hate I am the cause.

"I don't know what you see when you close your eyes, but I do know the woman I bound myself to."

His words make my heart sink. He loves the woman I was, not the woman I am. He loves a woman that might never come back.

"How could you? I don't even know the woman you

bound yourself to. You couldn't possibly know three hundred years of bullshit," I volley back as I sit up, clutching the sheet to my chest.

Fighting naked. Son of a bitch. If I had to count the number of times I desired to be fighting naked, that number would be less than zero.

"I know every machination and plot, I know every single stain you think you could have on your soul, and every single one was for others. You have never done a fucking thing for yourself. You have never—not once—done a damn thing for personal gain. Not. Once. So please, tell me, how you could ever think Iva's actions, Iva's machinations, Iva's endgame were your fault," Kyle rumbles, his voice trembles with the fight to stay calm. He still hasn't turned to face me, and it pisses me off more than his words do.

"It's tough to take you seriously when you won't even look at me when you say it," I murmur as I stand, snatching the rumpled sheet to wrap around my body, but as hard as I yank, I can't get it off one corner.

I should have forgotten the sheet and paid attention to the coiled-tight, six-foot-seven behemoth in the room because suddenly, I get half-tackled, half-thrown back on the bed. My yelp of surprise quickly turns into an oomph now that I have said behemoth laying right on top of me, his normally chocolate-colored eyes are coal-black from pupil to sclera with either lust, rage, or a little bit of both.

I should be scared, but I'm not. I know Kyle won't hurt me. I hate pissing him off, though. The gentle scrape of his talons scratches against my scalp as his hands cradle my face, and I have a hard time being the snotty little shit I've been acting like for the last few weeks.

"Let me try this again," Kyle growls through his fangs, "I know you. I know exactly who my wife is. You play the violin better than I have ever heard in three centuries. You can't cook for shit. You snore like a fucking grizzly bear. You are the most self-sacrificing woman I have ever met, and I think I hate and love that the most. You are not responsible for Iva. You earned your absolution ten times over because she can't terrorize anyone ever again. So stop feeling sorry for yourself, because the Nicola I know doesn't have time for self-pity. Got it?"

I search his face through watery eyes for a moment, trying to get myself under control when a banging at our front door shocks the shit out of both of us. Kyle's body goes from vibrating with pissed-off energy to rock-solid in an instant. He whips off of me grabbing my hand to pull me to standing.

"I thought the property was warded again?" I ask on

a fearful whisper, throwing on a bulky sweater over my braless chest and wriggle into skinnies.

No one should be knocking on our door. No one should even be able to see the fucking property. Kyle warded it against everyone. Hell, I don't even get a cell signal in this place. Kyle abandoned his Witch side at the start of our drama almost a year ago. He refused to use any kind of magic at all. He hated that part of himself. A part of me thinks he still might, but warding our home took priority over his ban on his Witch side.

"It was. I didn't feel anyone cross it," Ky replies as he buttons his jeans. "Can you see who it is?" he asks and I give him a look of bewilderment.

Does he expect me to get the door?

Then it dawns on me. He wants me to use the faulty power which doesn't seem to be back to anywhere close to full strength. Trust me, I've tried looking into the future—trying to see anything that could possibly happen. I've tried touching objects, chanting, meditation...

I see a whole lot of fuck all.

I give Kyle a look which expresses the depths of my skepticism before closing my eyes and pressing my mind outward. A needle of sharp agony blasts through my head and I see a flash of a face in my mind before my eyes snap open. I don't wait, I haul ass for the door, plowing into Kyle when he travels to intercept me, smoking out from our bedroom to the spot just before the front door.

"Who is it?" he says while he holds my hands away from the doorknob.

"Open the door, she's hurt!" I protest, wriggling out of his grasp and flipping the catch on the three deadbolts before ripping the door wide.

The tattered husk of a girl who is a bloody mess of rags on our front porch steals the breath from my lungs. She's propped up like a broken doll against a column, her head lolling to the side.

"Talia," I whisper, earning me a weak, watery smile from her before she passes out.

Grab Sight Kissed today!

BOOKS BY ANNIE ANDERSON

SEVERED FLAMES

Ruined Wings

IMMORTAL VICES & VIRTUES

HER MONSTROUS MATES

Bury Me

SHADOW SHIFTER BONDS

Shadow Me

THE ARCANE SOULS WORLD

GRAVE TALKER SERIES

Dead to Me

Dead & Gone

Dead Calm

Dead Shift

Dead Ahead

Dead Wrong

Dead & Buried

SOUL READER SERIES

Night Watch

Death Watch

Grave Watch

THE WRONG WITCH SERIES

Spells & Slip-ups

Magic & Mayhem

Errors & Exorcisms

THE LOST WITCH SERIES

Curses & Chaos

Hexes & Hijinx

THE ETHEREAL WORLD

PHOENIX RISING SERIES

(Formerly the Ashes to Ashes Series)

Flame Kissed

Death Kissed

Fate Kissed

Shade Kissed

Sight Kissed

Rogue Ethereal Series

Woman of Blood & Bone

Daughter of Souls & Silence

Lady of Madness & Moonlight

Sister of Embers & Echoes

Priestess of Storms & Stone

Queen of Fate & Fire

To stay up to date on all things Annie Anderson, get exclusive access to ARCs and giveaways, and be a member of a fun, positive, drama-free space, join The Legion!

facebook.com/groups/ThePhoenixLegion

Acknowledgments

A huge, honking thank you to Shawn, Barb, Jade, Angela, Heather, Kelly, and Erin. Thanks for the late-night calls, the endurance of my whining, the incessant plotting sessions, the wine runs... (*looking at you, Shawn.*)

Every single one of you rock and I couldn't have done it without you.

About the Author

Annie Anderson is the author of the international bestselling Rogue Ethereal series. A United States Air Force veteran, Annie pens fast-paced Urban Fantasy novels filled with strong, snarky heroines and a boatload of magic. When she takes a break from writing, she can be found binge-watching The Magicians, flirting with her husband, wrangling children, or bribing her cantankerous dog to go on a walk.

To find out more about Annie and her books, visit www.annieande.com

facebook.com/AuthorAnnieAnderson

instagram.com/AnnieAnde

amazon.com/author/annieande

bookbub.com/authors/annie-anderson

goodreads.com/AnnieAnde

pinterest.com/annieande

tiktok.com/@authorannieanderson